Autumn in August

With Best Wishes
Patricia Goodwin

Patricia Goodwin

First edition published by Silver Quill Publishing 2021

ISBN: 978-1-912513-89-5

UK spelling observed

Typeset in Georgia

Silver Quill Publishing

https://www.silverquillpublishing.com

To my children, with love

Chapter 1

Lucy shivered and pulled her coat higher round her neck It was a February morning, passengers were heaving luggage up the steps and across the bridge to the platforms on the other side of the station. The biting wind whipped down the railway line, whistling through the nooks and crannies making the bleakness of York station even more striking. Groups of bearded and long-haired young people and students, finding the waiting tedious, were either sprawled over what few seats were available or were squatting on their luggage. Strains of George Harrison's 'My Sweet Lord' drifted from a trannie. A few older people were shifting their weight from one leg to the other, stamping their feet and thrashing their arms in an effort to keep warm.

"Next train on platform 1 the 2.30 to King's Cross," came the disembodied voice over the tannoy. As the train approached the platform Lucy nestled closer to Richard. He put an arm gently around her shoulders. "Don't look so unhappy Mum, it's not the end of the world. I know you're upset now but three years will pass in no time and hey, you'll be able to come for a long holiday."

Since they had left home that morning Lucy had been very subdued. Richard was aware that, although his mother was pleased he had done so well in obtaining this posting, she was really sad at his leaving. He was wondering how his parents would cope without him and what effect it would have on their relationship and why he should be worrying about it; after all they were in good health and sound mind but being both observant and sensitive, he knew things were not as they should be. He was wondering too what was in store for him and whether he had made the right decision.

Lucy, trying hard to keep her emotions under control, replied,

"Yes, I know you're right, but I'll miss you so much."

She pulled away from his arms and as he towered over her, she stretched to full height. She threw her arms around his neck and gave him a last farewell kiss. Richard gently withdrew from her embrace and turned to his father. Lucy shrunk downwards.

Bob took a heavy draw on his pipe. The exhaled smoke, pronounced by the cold air, swirled upwards in rings. They had said their real goodbyes earlier.

"Cheerio old chap, have a safe journey and don't forget to keep in touch," he blurted as he gave Richard a fond but hearty slap on his back with one hand whilst clutching his pipe with the other. Richard had for some time now recognised that this was his father's prop. The smell of St. Bruno rough cut always permeated the house.

The train pulled out of the station. Lucy, coming to life again, waved, craning her neck to get that final glimpse of the receding figure, before it disappeared into the distance. Although stoical by nature, she was finding it hard not to give way to her feelings. She squeezed her eyes tightly but, nevertheless, a few tears trickled down her cheeks. She fumbled for a tissue in her pocket to hastily wipe them away before she turned to face Bob who seemed unperturbed and quite passive. Well, what else would she expect. Lucy thought that secretly Bob was not unhappy to see Richard go because now he would have her undivided attention. He had always been jealous of the attention she gave him and of her friends, too. Richard was their only child and Lucy doted on him, so parting was particularly difficult for her although she was, nevertheless, proud that he had secured such a good contract. But why did it have to be on the other side of the world?

"Come on cheer up. You have to let go sometime and the longer he stays at home the more difficult it will become. He is twenty-three after all and it's time he left home to stand on his own feet. Let's go for tea, a special treat at Betty's and then to see a film tonight. It might cheer us up. I think that one with Barbara Streisand and Robert Redford's on, 'The Way We Were.' You said you'd like to see it."

"OK. That sounds like a good idea. Appropriate title too," she mustered with a toss of her head.

"You sound as keen as a block of wood," he replied ignoring the dig.

***

It was the usual good old English summer that decided to

start quite late on in the season. The weather that everyone had anticipated for so long, until now, had eluded them. Lucy looked up at the clock, the one that they had been given as a wedding present, nearly twenty-five years ago. That day, Lucy not only made her marriage vows but promised herself that she would make her marriage a much happier one than that of her parents. The clock remained unchanged, but Bob had changed, and he was late again. Half past six, where was he? This was happening more frequently. She was beginning to resent spending so much time preparing food that he had become increasingly indifferent towards. Today she felt this even more keenly with the weather being particularly hot and clammy. A salad would have been more suitable than a hot meal, but Bob was not fond of them and she always endeavoured to please him. Lucy was becoming acutely aware that she had not fulfilled the promise she made to herself a quarter of a century ago. Put like that it seemed an age.

It had been a warm day and the evening was really for sitting out, so while she was waiting for Bob, Lucy poured herself a glass of wine and walked on to the terrace. She rummaged through the pile of chairs that had been hastily stacked and used only a couple of times since last season. They were a sad reminder of the sunny days of last year when she and Bob sat having a drink before their evening meal, making the most of the long light evenings. Leaves and dirt clung around the chairs, but Lucy managed to disentangle one of the more comfortable seats. She gave it a quick brush down, pulled it into the evening sunshine and sat looking on to the garden She cupped her hands around the glass of wine, savouring the bouquet, a Bordeaux, one of their favourite red wines which sparkled with an even redder glow as the sun gently kissed the glass. Marmalade, their ginger and white cat, jumped onto her, gently padding his paws on her thigh. He then turned himself round a few times and finally curled himself into a ball in the centre of her lap and purred loudly.

Children's voices echoed in the still evening air. With the comforting warmth of the sun, and the aroma of the wine, Lucy drifted back in time to some earlier recollections of her married life which had had its ups and downs but was certainly happier than the present. This had been the period following the Second World War when times were, by comparison, austere. They had very little money and some commodities were still rationed. Furnishing a small house was a struggle with the small amount of savings that they had managed to accumulate. There was little choice and what was available had the government's utility mark underneath. It was functional. But the birth of their son Richard had certainly put some happiness into their lives, at least into Lucy's. She knitted and sewed his clothes to help with her limited budget. She doted on him. He made her life worth living. Lucy would have liked another child, but it was not to be.

The loud and intrusive ringing of the telephone shattered the silence, disturbing her peace. Her first instinct was to let it ring but always fearing the worst, she felt compelled to answer in case some disaster had befallen Bob. Lucy thought, how strange is life that when we are happily engaged in something the telephone is a nuisance. It has an all-encompassing raucous sound resonating into every corner. When we are feeling lonely though, it can be a relief to have the silence broken, even with a wrong number call. The human voice is sometimes soothing, and the caller distracts the mind from sad or harrowing thoughts. Lucy recalled a particularly low point in her life when someone in distress had mistakenly dialled her number. 'I wonder if that poor chap did manage to contact his mother,' she mused. She remembered how she had tried to locate her but to no avail. She wished she had been able to help.

In her haste to answer the relentless ringing Lucy tripped and knocked over her glass of wine. Lifting her hands to her head in despair, she cried, "Oh dear, that's one of our best crystal glasses given as a wedding gift from one of Bob's past girlfriends, the one prior to Bella to whom he had been engaged and whose photo remained in his collection. Bob will be livid when I tell him. He'll say, 'you're so damned careless.'" Marmalade jumped down, weighed up the situation and decided to saunter off to a warm spot by the garden shed.

She left the wine dripping on to the terrace, went inside and picked up the phone, "Hi, Lucy here."

"I'm going to be another half hour or so. Keep the meal

warm," a voice blurted.

"Oh, it's you Bob. I'm so relieved."

Bob was obviously safe but at the same time, by the tone of his voice, she knew something was, indeed, wrong. It was sharp, and he normally would have asked her if she would mind keeping the meal hot. Something was up.

"Who in the hell did you think it would be. Perhaps you were expecting someone else?"

Raising her voice, Lucy answered,

"I'll treat that remark with the contempt it deserves. You know I always worry about you when you're late, wondering if something's happened to you. Why're you going to be late again?"

"Well why d'you think?" Bob's voice was getting louder and increasingly irritated.

"Work I suppose," Lucy offered meekly, her top lip beginning to quiver, for she knew in her heart this was not the truth. "OK, I'll keep the meal hot for you," she sighed.

"No point in getting upset. That's the way it is."

He replaced the receiver before Lucy could say any more. She sighed and made her way back to the terrace collecting a cloth and retrieving an old newspaper from the table. She carefully picked up all the pieces of the fragile glass, wrapped them in the newspaper, mopped up the wine and returned to the house to pour herself another drink. She felt something trickle down her hand and noticed that her finger was bleeding. She had accidentally cut it on a splinter of the glass. Drops of bright red blood dripped on to the floor as she went indoors to get a plaster. They mingled with the tears that she could not hold back, now large and plopping onto the floor, not because her finger hurt, but because of the situation that she knew she had to face. Lucy did not enjoy confrontation, but the problem had to be sorted. She hastily covered the cut with a plaster from the kitchen first aid box and once more sat down in the late evening sun wondering how she was going to broach the subject. A cold shiver ran up her spine as she thought about it.

The summer flowers were at their brightest. She watched a blackbird dip its beak into the pond to take refreshment in the pleasant evening air. It lifted and shook its head as if to say, well that's a lot better. Lucy loved the garden and her birds which she fed every day and she spent many hours watching them as they jostled for position on the bird table and pecked away at the seeds and nuts hanging alongside. They had moved to this leafy suburb of York twelve years ago. The structural engineering company that Bob worked for had procured a large contract just outside of the city and Bob was asked to take up the Manager's position. Richard had been very sad. "Do we have to go Mum? I don't want to leave all my pals."

"I'm afraid so Richard. Dad has had a promotion which means a lot more money."

"It's always Dad and what he wants. No thought for me."

"That's unfair Richard and you know it. You'll soon make new friends once you've settled into St Oswald's school."

"Well, I don't want new friends I'd rather keep my old ones." He banged the door as he left the room. Lucy sighed. They had to move where Bob's work took them. This house had been their best affordable option. Although it had needed a great deal of restoration, it had conjured a welcoming atmosphere and they immediately felt at home. Mr. and Mrs. Harris, the previous owners, had lived there happily all their married life but had become too frail to maintain such a large property. It was typical of the pre-war period. Lucy and Bob had thrown themselves into the project with a great deal of enthusiasm. They had lovingly recreated the garden too, which had taken a great deal of patience and effort to reach the very special place it had become. Richard had soon settled down, making new friends. All the while Richard remained at home the household, on the surface, was a happy one filled with children's laughter and fun.

As Richard grew older, he became introspective and spent many hours reading and studying in his room, leaving his mother and father to their own devices. This was when Lucy noticed a few cracks in their relationship begin to widen. Now that he had gone to Australia, they were spending much less time in the garden which not long ago had meant so much to them. Things felt different but she could not put her finger on it and perhaps did not really want to accept what she felt was inevitable.

Lucy had started working after they had moved to York. Up until that point Bob was adamant that she remained at home.

"I don't want a wife of mine having to earn money."

Then, unexpectedly, one evening on his return from work, opening a pile of bills he said, "I've been thinking it might be a good idea for you to take a job again." Lucy dropped the recipe book she was holding and stood with her mouth agape.

"Why this sudden change of heart?" Her voice was barely audible.

"We could do with some extra money to help with Richard's education and all these outstanding accounts which you seem oblivious to. I don't know where all the money goes."

Lucy was surprised on the one hand, but so happy on the other, she did not know whether to laugh or cry. At last to be able to leave the house and enjoy new friendships. She had enjoyed working at the insurance company where she had become a senior well-respected employee, until five years ago when she had been seriously ill and, after careful consideration, they agreed that it would probably be better if she did not return to full time employment. She had worked up the ranks establishing herself as personal assistant to the office manager and having to relinquish it made her desperately unhappy.

"Well, it's not the end of the world," said Bob on that miserable day five years ago after the party and farewells. "I think you'll enjoy not having to work. After all, ever since you started you said you never had time to do all the things you would like to do. The mortgage is paid and we could go for holidays without the worry of getting time off together."

It had been fine for a while, but she missed the buzz of the workplace and all the chit chat with her colleagues, with some of whom she was still in contact. Occasionally, she would open her wardrobe and look disconsolately at all her clothes that she no longer needed. Fashion conscious, she had dressed smartly and enjoyed a weekly visit to her hairdresser which she could no longer justify. She loved the casual lunches they enjoyed round the log fire at the Kings Arms and, during better weather, sitting on the green under the trees watching the pleasure cruisers going towards the Bishop's Palace. Occasionally, they might be lucky enough to see some of the university students practising for the boat race. Oh, for the enthusiasm and strength of youth. Those times regrettably had long gone and here she was feeling claustrophobic, caged. She had forfeited her independence.

It was more than a year ago that they had said goodbye to Richard, whose absence she felt more keenly as time wore on. Richard was an intelligent boy. He had a passion for books developed from his early years. She remembered how he shared his books with his friends. He always did well, first at school and then at university where he obtained a first-class degree with honours in civil engineering. Along with her work he was Lucy's world and reason for being. In the early days there had always been school functions, sports days and prize-giving events to attend, and she had played an active role on the Parents' Committee. Latterly, she ferried him to and from the station for vacations and he remained very much part of the family until he obtained his excellent posting in Australia. They were always ready to take well-qualified people; those who had much to offer. She was so proud and wished him well, but she felt empty. She knew instinctively that it had been Richard who, although in some ways had been partly responsible for their faltering marriage, had also helped to paper over the cracks. Lucy realised this was probably one of the reasons why things were now going badly wrong for them.

The phone rang again. 'Who is it this time,' she wondered. 'It seems that I'm not to enjoy the solitude of the early evening.' This time she was careful not to rush.

"Hello Lucy. How're you doing?"

It was Liz, a colleague with whom she once worked.

"Hello Liz. Well, you've caught me at a bad time. I'm not very happy at the moment. Bob's just rung to say he's going to be late again. I rushed to answer the call knocking over and breaking one of our best crystal wine glasses and cut my finger into the bargain. That's nearly every night this week he's been late. I just don't believe it's work. I'm sure he's seeing someone else. Our marriage has been rocky for some time as I've told you before, but more recently it's been going rapidly downhill. Something's up, I'm sure."

"Oh, I shouldn't worry too much. Marriages go through these phases. Things'll brighten up again. I expect he's having a hard time at the office. After all, it's a fairly boring existence for an intelligent man, working with that uninteresting bunch, you must admit."

"No more boring than mine is at present," replied Lucy with a hint of sarcasm in her voice.

"I have to go into town tomorrow. Managed to get a cancellation appointment with the chiropodist. I wondered whether you'd like to meet me and we could have lunch somewhere. It seems a while since we met up. You can off-load your troubles then if you'd like someone to talk to."

"OK, that sounds like a good idea."

Lucy was not too sure she wanted to let Liz know her deeply held concern for her marriage.

"I'll meet you then about eleven o'clock outside of Marks and Sparks."

"OK, Liz, I'll look forward to that," answered Lucy trying to sound a little brighter despite the fact that it was the last thing she felt like doing but did not wish to hurt Liz's feelings. After all she had known her for a long while.

They chatted a while longer, then Lucy remembered the meal, "I must go Liz. Make sure the dinner's not drying up."

"OK then, see you tomorrow. And cheer up."

***

Bob took his jacket from the peg. Turning to his secretary, he said,

"I'm going to a meeting and I won't be back today. If anyone phones take a contact number and tell them I'll return the call later."

Bob left in what seemed to be quite a hurry. Kate his secretary raised an eyebrow. This was uncharacteristic behaviour and there was nothing in the diary. Then she remembered he had received a telephone call earlier in the day when she could not help but overhear some rather heated exchanges. She thought maybe he and Lucy had fallen out over something. He had seemed rather subdued of late; also, he missed deadlines for quotations and was late for appointments and accounts were not paid. He slammed the door. Kate heard his footsteps clattering down the stairs and took a peek out of the window. Bob's shiny red sports car was parked just outside. He wasted no time in throwing his jacket on the back seat and driving off. The roar of the engine and screeching tyres indicated that it would be better if nobody was in his way.

As Bob neared the avenue in which Trish lived, he slowed his speed and, peering through the leafy trees, he located her flat which was one of eight in a conversion of a much larger property. As usual, not wishing to make his appearance too conspicuous, he drove well beyond the entrance and parked his car in a side road. He pulled a pipe from his pocket, scraped the debris loose in the bowl and gently tapped it into the ash tray. He slowly filled his pipe with fresh tobacco and lit it with a shiny new lighter that Trish had given him, which he then concealed in his glove compartment. He wound down the window and drew on his pipe enjoying the aroma of the freshly lit tobacco. He pondered for a while, wondering how he would approach Trish, then left his car. With a brisk pace and a determined look on his face he reached the house and took the flight of steps two at a time. He rang the bell and Trish opened the door expecting the usual welcome.

"Well, what's all this about then, ringing me at the office when I specifically asked you not to?"

Trish was taken aback. Where was the customary loving embrace and the long passionate kiss?

Holding her nose, she said, "I wish you wouldn't smoke that smelly pipe. It gives you away."

Bob extinguished his pipe, tapped it against the heel of his shoe then stuffed it into his pocket, "What on earth's the matter? I told you not to contact the office arousing suspicions."

"There's something we need to discuss, never mind the office protocols," she ventured.

"Surely it could have waited until tomorrow evening."

"No, 'fraid not. It rather concerns the here and now and our future."

"Future?" said Bob raising his voice, "We're not going through all that again. I won't leave Lucy yet. The time's not right. You'll just have to trust me and be patient a bit longer."

Pulling herself to her full height, and clenching her hands tightly by her sides, Trish replied through clenched teeth, "That's always your answer. This time it won't do. You have to make the decision. It's me or Lucy. No more clandestine meetings and love making."

"Well, if that's it then I'm off."

"That won't work." She stamped her foot becoming hysterical.

Bob stepped further inside, worried that passers-by would hear the commotion. He tried to pacify her, but she pushed him away.

"Now look, Trish, I can't just leave Lucy. I need time to sort things out."

"You've had plenty of time to sort things out, as you say. If you had any backbone you would've done it by now. You're cheating on both of us."

"I have to go now, but I promise I'll be back tomorrow evening and we'll talk things over."

He drew closer to her again and managed a peremptory kiss on her cheek.

"With your bags, don't forget. I've a stack of tablets upstairs ready if you don't keep your word and there's the gas oven too. Robert won't be impressed when he hears about it," she cried.

A face peered through the curtains from the flat above wondering no doubt what the noise was about. This worried Bob. He turned and hurried to the car without even a backward glance. He did not like to see Trish cry but neither did he wish to be identified. He sat in his car for a while considering his next move. He was fond of Trish but unsure whether he desired her sufficiently to make their relationship permanent. He was regretting the fact that he had taken advantage of her naivety for she believed he was in earnest. He thought suicide was an empty threat. From what she had revealed of herself, he did not think she was the suicidal type despite her show of hysteria.

Bob drove into town. He found a quiet bar and bought a beer which he hoped would help to steady his nerves. Trish was vulnerable and he felt protective towards her. He enjoyed the fact that she had become dependent on him for warmth and love.

This was how he felt about Lucy when he married her. It gave him a feeling of being needed. He worried about how Trish would react if she did not get her own way. She had regaled him with stories of her childhood which revealed that she had been brought up in a dysfunctional family and had experienced little love and affection from either of her parents. She had a number of siblings who had all been left very much to their own devices while growing up, but she had an older brother Robert who was overly protective towards her. Bob had no means of confirming these stories, but if true her brother could make his life difficult at work. He needed time on his own now, a kind of half-way house but how was he to approach Lucy, and some explanation would eventually have to be given to Richard.

Lucy heard Bob's car swerve into the drive. Should she tackle him about her suspicion or let sleeping dogs lie? They had parted that morning on bad terms, so Lucy decided not to say anything which she knew would inflame an already smouldering fire. What had started as a perfect evening was eclipsed by the signs of a thunderstorm.

Bob's steps to the house were much quicker than usual. He thrust the kitchen door open and deliberately banged his brief case on the table.

Turning to Bob, "I think there's a storm brewing," Lucy said, nonchalantly, as she replaced the pan on the hob and started to stir the heavily congealed sauce.

Gazing at her with cold eyes, he replied, caustically, "How did you guess?"

Turning her head towards him, "What's that supposed to mean?" answered Lucy, hesitantly. Unsure of what Bob was getting at, the stirring became slower. She wondered whether he guessed what she thought. He always seemed pretty good at weighing up people's feelings and assessing their reactions. Together with his cool and laid-back manner in the most difficult situations, this was, after all, something Lucy admired in Bob's character. This abrupt and somewhat blustery approach was alien to him, and Lucy thought quite rightly that something was amiss.

"You know very well what I mean. Our marriage is on the

rocks. Over the past months it's been nothing but a series of storms brewing up and boiling over. I'm just tired of it all and I'm leaving right now."

Lucy let go of the spoon which fell to the floor leaving blobs of sauce in its wake. She stood open-mouthed, incredulous. She knew things were not good but she had not realised that they had sunk to these depths. Bob stormed from the kitchen and up the stairs to the bedroom. He dragged two suitcases from the storage area, pulled open some drawers and hastily threw shirts and underwear into them not bothering to pack them neatly. Lucy followed in hot pursuit.

"Bob, have you taken leave of your senses?" she blurted out. She grabbed his arms and tried to stop him, but Bob simply shook her away and carried on determined not to be distracted from his decision. He closed the suitcases and as he did so, the old labels still tightly fastened to the handles caught his eye. They were a reminder of better times when they had spent a wonderful month touring around Italy. Bob could not allow these sentiments to get in the way, so he hastily blocked them from his mind before he could change it as he tossed his suits into a suit carrier.

"I told you I am going. I've had enough. It's time to call it a day or are you too dumb to realise neither of us are happy? I'm moving out, now."

Barely able to speak, her voice came in a hoarse whisper,

"Well, what about the dinner? I've kept it warm," she asked simply, standing like a limp rag doll as though some angry child had just vented its spite on her by giving her a good shake. Bob was at the end of his tether.

"That just about sums you up. An important event like a failing marriage and all you can think of is your precious dinner. Well, what about it? Insignificant in view of the situation I would've thought."

"At one time a dinner would've been very important to you, especially if you were entertaining some of your high and mighty business associates. What's happened to them? Have they all deserted you? It wouldn't surprise me if you are no more civil to them than you have been to me recently," yelled Lucy who was beginning now to rise to the occasion and was in danger of losing control. She tried to stop the tears that were stinging her eyes again and were threatening to tumble down her cheeks and collect in large drops on the end of her nose. She snuffled into her handkerchief.

"Here we go. Well, the blubbering won't work this time," stormed Bob.

She was beginning to understand the real reason behind Bob's uncharacteristic behaviour of late.

"So this is the reason then behind the long evenings you've spent alone listening to music and reading in your study excluding me from as much of your life as possible. Late evenings, disinterest in food that I foolishly attributed to stress and overwork. How wrong can one be and how you have fooled me. Who is it then? Someone I know?" Lucy spluttered between bouts of near screams and tears.

"I am not going to live with anyone else."

Her voice gradually rising, she answered, "That's not the same thing as saying there isn't anyone, is it?"

"Well, we've never talked to one another openly about important issues. They've always been brushed under the carpet. You've never been interested in my work or pastimes. You've only ever had time for Richard or some friend like Marjorie who incidentally had a lot more going for her than you have."

Lucy did not pick up on this remark but thought it more than a little odd. Marjorie had left some years ago when Richard was about eight years old. Bob was cool as he stuffed socks and underwear into his case, but Lucy could feel the bitterness in his voice. It was if he had bitten into a sour plum and was not able to spit it out. She was distraught.

"I've learned over the years not to confront you or try to discuss anything because you always closed up like a clam and I was afraid you'd drive off and leave me alone like you used to."

They had had disagreements early in their marriage over money matters and how Richard should be disciplined. He would drive off and leave her exasperated, wondering whether he would return and, if not, how would she cope on her own; worse still, the reaction of his parents in whose eyes he could do no wrong. He had always come back though, but a difficult time would ensue when neither of them wished to accept responsibility for the situation or make amends. A contemptuous silence reigned; a kind of truce would evolve after a long period with only the minimum amount of communication; more layers of silence, then they would gradually fall back into the same old groove until the next episode. In her heart, Lucy wondered whether he would drive off now and return after some thinking time, but her head told her otherwise; besides which, he had never before packed a suitcase or said that he was leaving. This was different.

Bob completed his packing and, as he stormed out of the house, called,

"Don't get any ideas that I might come back. This is for good."

He slammed the door behind him, as he made his way to his car, almost knocking Lucy off balance, but she jumped back in time. She raced after him and, opening the passenger door, as he turned the ignition, asked lamely,

"Where are you going to stay and how can I get in touch with you?"

"There you go again with your stupid remarks. I don't know where I'm going and if I did, I wouldn't tell you because that's the whole point of going... or didn't you realise?" He accelerated the car in a rage and, with a roar, tyres spinning spitting gravel everywhere, he drove off. Lucy feared for his safety. She clutched her balled handkerchief, by now sodden with tears, and eyes lowered to the ground lest she stumbled, she made her way back into the house. She tried hard to think what had led to this disastrous state of affairs. Was there anything she could have done to prevent it, she asked herself as she sunk into the nearest armchair? Where was the tall, debonair man, always in control, never overtaken by events, the good raconteur with grossly exaggerated tales, all part of his charm that had attracted Lucy to him? Lucy had to acknowledge, though, that since Richard's birth a rather uncompromising streak occasionally appeared which gave way to a hasty show of temper that exploded like a champagne cork bursting from its bottle, but the fizz soon dissipated; nothing like she had just witnessed. She knew he was jealous of the attention she gave Richard. Reflectively, she admitted to herself, perhaps he had a point. At one time this would have been inconceivable to her, but a wedge had certainly been driven between them. But why this unseemly display of temper now? After all, Richard was no longer with them. There had to be something else, another woman, of that she was sure. This felt like the Autumn of their marriage. The marriage that had weathered so many storms but, as winter approached, had eventually floundered and broken like a ship, wrecked and washed up on the shore.

By late evening Lucy had managed to pull herself together. She busied herself salvaging the meal and putting things straight, but she was not able to make sense of the events of the last hour or so. Everything had taken place so quickly. She went to bed, but sleep would not come; she kept turning it all over in her mind wondering what her next step should be. At two o'clock she was still tossing and turning, the space beside her which Bob had filled with his warm body, was gaping and cold. She went downstairs to make a drink of hot chocolate, perhaps that would soothe her jangled nerves. She sipped her drink and turned to put out the light, wondering where and with whom Bob was sleeping, and eventually drifted into a very fitful sleep.

When Lucy woke she remembered that she had arranged to meet Liz that morning. 'Oh, I would much rather stay in bed, I really don't feel like going out' she thought but decided she could not let Liz down. She had after all been a good friend and this was a time when she might need a shoulder to lean on. She dragged herself from her bed and took a shower and hastily put on the first clothes that she came across. She tried to disguise the black rings under her red and swollen eyes with concealer. It seemed to make little difference, but Lucy was late and past caring. She grabbed her bag and car keys, left the house and drove into town.

She parked her car and made her way to their designated meeting point.

"Hello," called a voice from across the road.

Liz waved her arms frantically to attract Lucy's attention.

"I thought we could go for a drink and a bite to eat. My, you certainly look as though you could do with a stiff drink of some sort."

"I nearly put you off but then decided I would burst if I stayed in the house all day alone. Bob and I had the most terrible row and he has walked out."

"Oh, I'm sure he'll be back. He's not the sort to do anything so rash."

"Maybe, but I think it is for real this time."

Lucy did not go into detail about her experience and left it there.

She had a drink but declined to eat anything. Liz was concerned and, before they parted, told her that she could ring any time if she needed to talk.

Chapter 2

Bob had found himself some temporary accommodation where he could be alone to sort out his life. He had met Trish at an annual dinner dance held by his company to give employees, from all their branches, the opportunity to meet on a friendly level. She was with a group of girlfriends and Bob, always ready to spot a pretty girl, found himself beguiled by her lovely smile and large innocent eyes. The warmth she exuded and the happiness that shone from her eyes reminded him so much of Marjorie. She was fresh and charming.

Bob sauntered to their table while Lucy was enjoying a dance with one of the directors.

Bob held out his hand and asked, "Would you like to dance?"

Trish was soon on her feet.

"What's a lovely young lady like you doing here, unaccompanied?" Bob was good at inveigling information from the opposite sex.

"Ah well, I was divorced and then met another fellow and we were engaged but he had second thoughts, didn't he, and broke off our engagement," was her reply as she dropped her eyes and squeezed a tear. Bob took her to the bar, bought her a drink where they chatted until the music changed again. They had the next dance together during which time Bob had discovered where she worked and what time she went for lunch.

"Are you on your own?"

"No, but I might as well be. That's my wife in the green silk gown enjoying herself with that suave dark-haired fellow." Trish felt a warmth that she had never experienced before as Bob placed his arm around her waist and guided her back to her girlfriends.

On the following Friday he made his way to the coffee bar where he knew she would have gone for her lunch. "What a surprise to see you here. D'you come here often?" she asked as he made his way to her table.

"Oh, now and again and today is my lucky day."

Trish was uncertain whether it was by accident or design

that he was there, but whichever, she was pleased to see him.

Bob's meetings with Trish became more frequent. He was enjoying the company and none of the responsibility that accompanied a permanent relationship. He made love to her as often as he could find an excuse to get away. It was not long before he discovered the error of his ways. Trish was not going to be happy with being available to suit Bob but was determined to make the relationship on her terms. Bob, acutely aware of the emotional vacuum in his marriage, soon felt trapped. This had led to the final snap.

Trish discovered that Bob had left Lucy and in the ensuing weeks she would not leave him alone. The situation was becoming intolerable. His nerves were raw and shattered and he feared, if he did not exercise some kind of order, he would lose his job. He finally gave way and moved in with Trish. It was not a happy time for either of them, both seeking each other for the wrong reasons. They had bitter rows. Bob soon began to realise that Trish was not the ineffective, dependent person she made herself out to be. After a few turbulent months he had become suspicious that Trish's former fiancé was visiting. She denied this but Bob returned from the office early one Friday afternoon and found that they had been in bed together. He heard a scuffle above and seething with rage made for the stairs only to be met by her fiancé emerging from the bedroom, in his underpants, clutching his shoes.

Bob pushed passed the fellow who grabbed the rail to steady himself. "Get the hell out of here," he yelled as he picked up the trousers that lay in a heap where they had been dropped. He hurled them out of the window; "Here you forgot these," and turned to Trish, "What sort of a person are you, breaking up a marriage and placing me in an impossible position. What the bloody hell for – fun? You little slut," he almost spat at her.

He was angry with himself as much as with Trish for allowing himself to be duped.

"You told me your marriage was over. That's what they all say isn't it and the baby I'm carrying isn't even yours anyway," Trish screamed. Bob had to admit to himself that his marriage was over, but baby... what baby? He was as certain as he could be that he was not the father of any baby. He also doubted that Trish was pregnant, but it was a complication he could well do without.

"You'd better get your ginger-haired lover to move back with you then."

"His name is Freddie," she snarled curling her lip.

Bob left in high dudgeon. Freddie did in fact move back and much to Bob's relief it eventually became obvious that there was no baby.

Some months passed. Bob did not contact Lucy and refused to speak to her when she rang the office. Kate, Bob's secretary, either knew nothing of what he was doing or where he was living or she had been told not to disclose his whereabouts. Lucy finally gave up trying.

Then one afternoon a fresh event surfaced. The telephone rang. Lucy answered, thinking it would be her friend, but she was taken aback to hear Bob's voice.

"Hello, how are you?"

"Oh, it's you Bob. Well, do you really care?" Lucy asked.

"As a matter of fact I do, which was one of my reasons for leaving in the first place. There's no point in trying to continue in a marriage if one partner doesn't love the other. It's doomed as has been proved."

"Well, come to the point. Which one of us doesn't love the other?"

Bob ignored the question.

"I want a divorce," he went on. "It's time to move on and get on with our lives. I'm willing to provide the grounds. I've been in touch with a solicitor but of course it's up to you."

"So that's it. I suppose I should have guessed."

"It's not what you think but then I can't blame you after the way I behaved towards you."

"So you're coming cap in hand then. A bit late for remorse now."

"I know I left in haste, but I had thought about it for a long time. I decided it was the best way forward and the only way I could summon the courage was to do it quickly. There was never any hope of me turning back and that remains so today, whatever you decide. Anyway, mull it over. I will of course pay any costs involved. I suggest that in future it'll be easier for us both to make representations through our respective solicitors."

"What do you mean, 'mull it over'? You're the one who should be mulling things over as you say. Remember, you were the one who left in haste without offering a sensible reason or even giving me the opportunity to discuss the situation. You have refused to speak to me and not even had the grace to reply to my requests and you have the gall to ask me to 'mull it over'. What's happened to your little bit on the side, then, who you shacked up with, or is it just a spiteful rumour? Has she left you now?"

With that she put down the phone.

Lucy froze; what a bombshell Bob had dropped. She collapsed into the nearest chair. She clutched her throat as she started gasping and felt her pulse racing. She wobbled as her legs turned to jelly when she tried to stand. She was unable to move. Lucy was overwrought because in her heart she had hoped that this was a time for reflection; time for a bit of space, that eventually they would get back together again. Desolation crept over her. The physical situation had not changed, they were no longer together but the last tiny ray of hope had been stolen from her; the little ray of hope that she clung to and which had kept her going. She felt so unloved and lonely. She stared through the window until the night clouds began to gather. The moon hovered over, offering a stark intermittent light. She shivered and suddenly a pang of hunger forced its way into her knotted stomach, but the thought of food made her feel nauseous. Beginning to feel very cold, Lucy draped the rug from the back of the chair around her shoulders and drew her feet underneath her body. She drifted into an uneasy sleep. She was awakened later by Marmalade jumping on to her. He was hungry too. She stroked his silky coat, which gave her some comfort, and he purred in recognition. He meowed, as if to say, "Now please get me my dinner."

Lucy dragged herself from the chair, but she was unable to stand immediately because both her legs were numbed as a result of sitting in such an awkward position. She sat for a while, rubbing some warmth into them. They gradually came to life. She pushed her feet into her mules and shuffled to the kitchen. She opened a new tin of cat food for Marmalade, the smell of which made her retch. She made herself a strong cup of coffee. She held the cup with both hands and sipped the drink. As the heat seeped through her body, her mind began to thaw. What will I do now she asked herself? She had one or two friends but at this stage Lucy was uneasy about letting anyone know. She felt such a failure and just wanted to curl up and die. Apart from Richard, she had no close relatives to talk to. She was disinclined to tell Richard at this stage because it would worry him. In any case he was too far away to be of any help.

Now, had Marjorie still been around she would most certainly have confided in her. She and Marjorie had struck up a friendship when their children were small, some fifteen years ago. Marjorie had twin boys, both with a head of curly hair. 'My, how time flies,' she said to herself. 'Such happy days.' Parents gathered at the school gates to meet their children and one such day Richard rushed to the gates closely followed by the twins.

"Mum, James and Josh have asked me to have a look at their new Hornby train set. Please let me go. I'd love to see it."

The twins always seemed a happy pair of children. They were instantly recognisable with their mop of ginger curly hair, and freckled faces.

Marjorie, their mother, approached Lucy.

"Hello, I'm the twins' mother. That sounds a nice idea. How about you come too, for a cup of tea?" she asked, "Our boys always seem to come out of school chatting together so it'd be quite good for them to play at home some days."

Lucy readily accepted. Finding themselves with much in common, they began to see each other quite regularly. They spent many afternoons over cups of coffee and tea, putting the world to rights while the children played happily. The twins were in awe at Richard's wonderful collection of books.

"Mum, have you seen all Richard's books? James asked his mother one afternoon as he looked with envy at them in the bookcase.

"You can borrow them in exchange for me playing with your

trains if you like, but promise you'll look after them," Richard volunteered.

"Oh thanks," replied James. " Sure we'll take care of them. We only get books from the school library. They're usually dog-eared, too."

"I'm lucky my Dad takes me to the big library in town every week, as well as buying me books."

"Wish ours did," answered James. "He's too interested in booze to take us anywhere."

Marjorie laughed off the comment but knew it was true.

Occasionally Marjorie and Lucy went on shopping expeditions. This was the time when the supermarkets had come to town. How everyone welcomed them; all the shopping under one roof, so convenient. Marjorie had an eye for good clothes. She helped Lucy build a small wardrobe of clothes using her limited budget to the best advantage. Bob always grumbled about her wasting money, especially if she bought new clothes for herself or Richard but not books.

Lucy and Bob were renting a large, detached house, their second married home in a small town near Liverpool where Bob had been posted to manage construction works. Marjorie's husband, Tom, was self-employed. They owned their own house and were a little more affluent. One afternoon Marjorie was quite excited. Over a cup of tea, she asked, "Would you like to join us on a holiday? Tom's parents have a lovely villa down in Cornwall which they let out during the holiday season. They're willing to let us have it for a couple of weeks. It'd be great fun. Better still, it won't cost us anything. There are beautiful beaches, sandy coves and the surf's good too, if you like that kind of thing."

"Oh gosh, thanks! That sounds wonderful. Not sure about the surfing but I like to swim. Richard would love it too. I'll see what Bob thinks tonight and let you know."

At this time most people could only afford day trips to the seaside or at best a week in a Butlin's holiday camp in a seaside resort. Therefore, to spend two weeks in a villa with minimum expense was more than a dream.

Lucy could hardly contain her excitement when Bob arrived home that evening.

"How would you like a holiday with Marjorie, Tom and the children in Cornwall?"

"Are you serious? You know we can't afford a holiday, never mind at the other end of the country."

"It won't cost us anything for the accommodation. A holiday would be good for us all, especially Richard."

As soon as the words were out of her mouth, she regretted saying them.

"Ah yes, Richard. Why is he in need of a holiday?"

"It will do us all good to get away for a while, change of scenery, recharge the batteries."

"Who is this Tom anyway? I don't really know him and I've only met Marjorie a few times. Then only briefly. She appears pleasant enough though. Has a lovely smile."

"I don't know Tom well. He's just a bit quiet. Doesn't have a lot to say. He does a lot of driving so I guess he gets tired. Bob, just consider it," she clasped her hands together, "It would be wonderful to have a proper holiday. I'm sure Tom'll be fine. Marjorie wouldn't have asked us if she thought he would be difficult."

" OK, I'll give it some thought."

Despite Lucy's reassurances Bob had a feeling that there was something odd about Tom. Nevertheless, after much discussion and persuasion that evening, after Richard had gone to bed, Bob reluctantly agreed. "We'll give it a whirl then, but you'll have to draw in your horns with finances. We'll have to save some money. There won't be any luxuries between now and then."

The next day, bubbling with excitement, Lucy told Marjorie that they would love to accept the invitation.

That summer they spent a happy fortnight in Cornwall. The children built sandcastles, watching with disappointment as the incoming tide washed them away. They splashed in and out of the water and played hide and seek in the sandy coves, too.

Marjorie was an extrovert character with sparkling eyes that lit up her face. She liked to flirt, which had not gone unnoticed by Bob. Lucy did have an inkling that Marjorie may have made a few overtures towards Bob but she was confident that Bob would not respond.

“Shall we walk the children along the beach?” she asked him as she tossed her mane of blond hair and flickered her eyelashes, one morning during that holiday, “The others seem to be preoccupied discussing politics which I find totally boring.”

“OK. Nice morning for it.”

Bob noticed how her hips swayed as she walked drawing attention to her petite but shapely figure, immaculately turned out. She generated a warmth, sadly lacking, Bob mused, in his marriage. He found her almost irresistible.

***

One morning, sometime after their holiday, over coffee Marjorie seemed very depressed. “Tom won’t let me buy a new dress,” she burst. “You know, I’m not really happy. He’s so mean with money and he hates me to buy new clothes or things for the house. He likes to take me for expensive dinners and dances with his wealthy clients but begrudges me the money to buy a new dress for the occasion. He doesn’t seem to understand it's degrading to keep wearing the same outfits. I’d like another baby too, a little girl would be wonderful after the twins, but Tom doesn’t want the expense. Ha, less for cigarettes and booze.” Lucy recalled the comment that James had made about his father. Once she did go as far as saying she could never leave Tom because she could never live without her boys. She could not consider taking them away because Tom would fight tooth and nail for them, aided by his parents. Lucy thought this was a strange thing for Marjorie to say, especially as she appeared to have quite an exciting lifestyle compared to hers. Perhaps there was something underlying this remark that Marjorie had not disclosed.

Once Lucy began to know Tom a little better, she discovered what a selfish character he was underneath that quiet persona. She had not been aware of just how difficult life really was for Marjorie until one day her mother-in-law rang. She was very distressed.

“Have you any idea where Marjorie is? She's not been home for two nights now She’s gone. Just walked out leaving Tom and those beautiful boys. They're here with me at the moment. She hasn’t left an address or any indication of where she might be.

We've asked other members of the family and friends if they have seen her but no one seems to know anything, not even her mother. You see a lot of her. I wonder whether you could throw any light on the situation. We're beside ourselves with worry. She just left a scribbled note to tell the children that she loved them very much and they would understand when they were older. She took some clothes with her, so she's obviously not intending to return. It's a total mystery. There have been rumours that someone had seen her walking along the tow path. Tho' the fact that she took clothes with her seems to suggest that she wasn't really meaning to take her life. The police are not ruling anything out at this stage. They're treating it as a missing persons case but we can't give them any leads. We're distraught," she snivelled, her voice breaking.

"Oh my word, that's dreadful news." Lucy unravelled the telephone cable which had a habit of knotting up, and went on, "Please don't cry. I was thinking about giving her a call because I hadn't seen her for a while which is unusual. I know nothing about her leaving except to say that she wasn't happy, particularly with financial matters, but she's never indicated that she would leave. In fact quite the contrary. I'm sure she'll come back. She'll come to her senses. Marjorie loves her children too much to leave them. Is there anything that I can do to help? P'raps they would like to come here after school for a few days until things get sorted. Richard did say that the twins hadn't been round for a while so this would be a good opportunity."

"That's very kind. It would be helpful and I'm sure they'd like it. Take their minds off things although we haven't yet told them everything in case she does return. It's not helping their grandfather's condition either. He's supposed to be kept quiet and stress free since his last heart attack. That's impossible with two boys in the house. It's all so distressing and selfish of Marjorie too. We did have an argument that morning over money matters but nothing that would warrant such behaviour."

"I'm sure it's very upsetting but unlike Marjorie to behave so selfishly. Look we'll expect the children after school if that will ease the situation and if I hear anything it goes without saying that I'll tell you straight away. You go and make yourself a nice cup of tea. It will calm your nerves. I have to go now. Don't forget to let me know if you have any news." With that she replaced the receiver. "Oh get down, Mufty." She pushed away a rather restless black dog of the proverbial Heinz variety. " All right, we'll go for a walk." She took down his lead and off they went across the fields. In her mind she was beginning to turn over recent conversations and events. She was puzzled. Why would Marjorie leave without telling her? It all seemed rather odd, and she was a little hurt that Marjorie did not tell her she intended to leave Tom. After all they had shared so much. Maybe Marjorie thought it would make life difficult for her and she would be obliged to tell the family where she had gone. Perhaps it was an impulsive decision. Nevertheless, she was puzzled and thought about Marjorie's earlier conversation which began to make some sense.

Bob was quite distressed that evening when Lucy told him what had happened. "Marjorie has gone? Gone where?"

"Well, if they knew they wouldn't have called the police." He fidgeted with the newspaper and pushed away his meal, "I don't feel like eating." It was a serious situation, but she did think he was overreacting. But with three children to look after instead of one she had more immediate problems to cope with and she chose to believe that the little niggles she felt were just fantasy. Time moved on. Richard saw less and less of the twins after their mother had left. Lucy and Bob moved further North but before they left Tom told Bob that Marjorie had asked him for a divorce. As a result she was traced to Canada but she refused to have any direct contact with him or her children. Tom moved away in an effort to bury the past and the two families eventually lost touch.

***

It was late August and it really felt like the Autumn of their marriage. After Bob's unexpected request, Lucy decided that it would be in her best interests to consult a solicitor who would give good advice and help with her next move. She went to the drawer in the large pine dresser which was something akin to Aladdin's Cave. Housed in one of its capacious drawers were two large telephone directories, address books and many other bits and pieces that they had collected over the years, including an old sweet tin. She hesitated then picked it up and shook it. As the coins inside rattled a smile broke over her face. That tugged at her heart strings but remembering what she had come for she replaced the lid and carefully put the tin back in the drawer. With trembling fingers, she pulled out the yellow pages and opened it at 'Solicitors'. Her eyes lighted on what seemed like an appropriate name. Tentatively, she picked up the phone, aware that this was a huge step she was about to take. She made an appointment for the following morning. 'Best to get it over as quickly as possible,' she mumbled to herself.

It was with some trepidation that Lucy kept the appointment the next day. She had spent the whole of the previous evening thinking about what she was going to say. 'What should I say in these circumstances?' she wondered. 'And what should I wear.'

Lucy found the offices in a rather grand villa which, in years past, she was sure would have been home to quite a wealthy middle-class family. With a newly found confidence she tripped up the steps and entered the front door where she was greeted by a very smart receptionist who asked her to take a seat. After what seemed an eternity Lucy was ushered into a room. A young-looking, fresh-faced fellow, or at least that was Lucy's impression, with a shiny complexion, trendy hairstyle and dapper suit rose from behind a very imposing desk. He shook her hand and indicated to her to sit down. She feared he had little knowledge of real-life situations which now gave her reservations about her choice of solicitor. Lucy began to lose her nerve; the large, oak desk between them made the situation very formal. She suddenly blurted out her whole story. All she really needed was someone who would listen.

"Well, Mrs Barber, what do you want to do?" was all he said.

"I don't know," came the reply, "That's why I have come for help."

"Well, I'm afraid I can't tell you whether or not you should agree to a divorce. I suggest you go away and think about it a little longer. Come back when you've made up your mind and we'll go through the procedures open to you if that is what you decide to do."

This was not what Lucy had expected. She was hoping someone would tell her what to do, or at least help her to make up her mind by weighing up the alternatives. Thoroughly bewildered, she left. She was no further forward with making a decision. Her first instinct she thought had been correct. Lucy consulted a second solicitor. As she eyed him up and down, she thought he looked more like a retired rugby player with his excessively padded frame. He was older and therefore probably more experienced but a ruddy complexion boasting myriads of tiny burst blood vessels suggested too much alcohol. He raised his eyes from a document and, peering over the top of his spectacles at her, with his nose almost touching his desk, and with a voice seemingly coming from his boots, simply said,

"Go ahead. He's obviously ready to move on and even if you patch things up now the situation will inevitably arise again."

Lucy was as taken aback with this advice as she had been with the first and considered it a simplistic way of looking at the situation, but at least he had listened and expressed an opinion. She spent another very restless night pondering everything but concluded that she would prefer to wait the two years before making any decision, when she would reconsider and maybe go ahead with their mutual consent. It was too great a change to make under what she thought was duress. Although attitudes surrounding divorce were becoming more socially acceptable, Lucy was not sure that it was where she wanted to be.

During this time Lucy did some soul searching. She wondered why their marriage had reached rock bottom without either of them acknowledging, until now, the depths to which it had plunged. She knew that Richard had come between them, but she could not help dragging her thoughts back to the fateful day before their marriage when Bob had been so angry with her for reading the letters she had received from Patrick. She wondered whether this had been a factor in causing Bob's jealous streak to develop. Prior to their wedding she remembered that she had had some doubts as to whether she had been too hasty in agreeing to the marriage, but it had been too late to turn back. Everyone would have been so angry with her, especially her father who had already expressed his reservations about her choice of husband. He never ceased to remind her how he could ill afford the grand wedding which they both expected. She supposed time would erase those remaining feelings but perhaps they continued to swirl around in her subconscious, occasionally surfacing from the depths of her heart. Perhaps they had never really left her but no, surely this was just her imagination running wild. No matter how hard she tried to rationalise the situation, the nagging doubt remained, and she recognised it was possible that Bob could have filled a gap for her. Too much had happened since then and she must not allow these thoughts to take hold. She was almost talking herself into that situation but more importantly now, she must turn herself to survival without Bob. Despite this, she never gave up hope that one day he would return.

Chapter 3

Whatever feelings Lucy had for Bob, and however hopeful she had been of patching up their marriage, she could not forgive him for what he had done. After two years their divorce was made absolute. Lucy was determined that this was not going to ruin the rest of her life. During this period she had grown tired of aimlessly filling her time and now that her health was no longer an issue, she felt it was right to look for some employment. This would not only keep her occupied but would make her financially independent of Bob. She wanted to make a clean break. With her share of the assets she decided to purchase a small property in another location. It was inevitable that she would eventually have to move to where she found employment. This is how she found herself in a small market town in North Yorkshire.

It was not the easiest of times to be seeking employment at her age, but Lucy had visions eventually of picking up her nursing career. She had always regretted giving it up but it had not been possible when Richard was younger. Now was a golden opportunity. Caring for the sick, whether humans or animals, had always been in her heart. But for the immediate future she needed something to bring in a small income. This proved to be quite difficult because everyone required experienced applicants. It was a catch twenty-two situation. How could one gain experience without the job? Nevertheless, undeterred, Lucy continued to scour the situations vacant columns in both local and national newspapers. She looked down at her dress grubby with ink from newsprint and turned over her blackened hands, another day of disappointment. It seemed there was not a lot left to life now, nothing to get up for. Then one morning something caught her eye. A nursing agency in London was looking for new recruits to assess suitable people for their books. Nursing qualifications were essential. Without delay, Lucy sent for an application form which she completed and returned promptly. Within a few days she had been given a date for an interview. London, she mused, would be different. Lucy was so excited. She needed to tell someone about her good news.

Recently, she had been contacted by one of her nursing contemporaries who had also been a schoolfriend. Mary had invited her to stay with them. Lucy remembered Mary as a tall slender figure always preening her jet-black, wavy hair in front of the mirror. Her parents ran an antiques business in the North and had been quite well off. Mary, an only child, wanted for nothing. Lucy envied the beautiful clothes she wore and wished so much that she had enough money to buy fashionable clothes. Now that the austerity from the war years had begun to lift there were such exciting new designs, like the 'New Look', coming into the shops. She remembered too, the pangs of guilt she suffered when drawing out the modest amount of post office savings that her beloved grandmother had passed to her on leaving school. Her grandparents had had a small farm. Lucy realised now how difficult it must have been for them to save money for her which she had frittered on clothes.

Lucy was an only child too but was from a modest background. Her father was a labourer. As was usual in those days her mother stayed at home. Her father held strong Socialist views, was a member of the Labour Party and did not really approve of her marriage to Bob, a staunch Conservative Party member.

"Don't you be getting too big for your shoes mind and get ideas above your station," he warned. "Money's hard to come by you know and you're expecting this grand wedding. Well, you've made your bed and you'll have to lie on it. It won't be any good to come crying back home if it doesn't work out."

Her parents were not happily married. Lucy remembered hearing constant rows after she had gone to bed, which usually occurred after her father had returned from the pub. He was not a heavy drinker, but her mother suspected he was seeing other women. Sometimes she taunted her father and provoked him into a rage. Once she remembered he picked up his dinner and threw it at the wall where some of it stuck, the remainder dropping into a greasy mess on the linoleum. Lucy knew that he was proud of her, although he would never tell her so. He had wanted her to do well at school but not too well. It would not be wise to have too much ambition because he liked to be in charge. She found her mother more amenable, but she sensed a jealous streak which her father played on. Lucy wished so much that she had an older brother or even a younger one would do, someone in whom to confide. "Why can't I have a brother or sister?" she would ask her mother when she was young.

"We've only just enough money for you, so another baby is out of the question."

She loved to get away from this conflict to spend time with her grandparents.

She had such fond memories of times spent on the farm, bringing in the cows for milking, collecting eggs, carrying warm rich creamy milk in a can for tea and watching butter being churned in the dairy. Many afternoons she had walked with her grandfather to bring in the cows for milking. He gave them all names.

"Come on Primrose," he would call gently patting her backside to hurry her along.

"Whoa there, Bluebell, not so fast," stretching his arms to prevent the cow from straying. Her Grandfather always walked at the same pace with a stick fashioned from the hedge row at the top of which he had cut a large notch for his thumb. He herded the cows into the milking parlour and secured them in their separate booths. The friskiest cow was milked first. He carried his three-legged milking stool in one hand and a bucket of warm water with a cloth in the other. Before Grandfather started to milk the cows, he carefully washed the teats that protruded from the cow's milk-swollen udders. He sat close to the cow with his forehead pressed against the cow's belly and a clean bucket between his legs. The milk made a whooshing noise which was rhythmic as it hit the bucket. Most of the cows were placid. But in the hot weather, when the flies were busy, they swatted them with their tails having no regard for the milker. Lucy collected the milk can from the house as they passed and returned with it filled with warm creamy milk. She helped her grandmother feed the hens and collect eggs too.

"Come on, let's find a nice brown egg for your tea."

She loved a soft-boiled egg with bread-and-butter soldiers

to dip into the deep yellow yolk which, as she pushed in the spoon, would spill down the side of the eggcup.

The chickens all squawked as they put their hands in the nesting boxes to look for eggs and when Grandmother tossed the corn from a small basket, they all gathered around fighting and pecking for the golden seeds that lay scattered on the ground. These were the times when Lucy began to develop her caring skills.

It was a sad time for Lucy when her grandparents died within a short time of each other soon after Richard's birth. Six months later, her mother, while on a day trip with the Women's Institute, was killed when their coach was involved in a collision with an articulated lorry. Poor Lucy thought her world was coming to an end, but she had Richard. 'Strange,' she thought, 'I did not think, well, I still have Bob.' Her father had remarried, and she became estranged from him. She neither liked nor was liked by his second wife, Judith.

Lucy picked up the phone and Mary's cheery tone was in keeping with her own feelings when she answered,

"Hello, Mary Birtwhistle here."

"Hello it's Lucy. I can't contain my excitement. Had to tell someone. I've been called to London to a nursing agency for an interview," she blurted out almost stumbling over her words.

"London! Why ever London?" exclaimed Mary.

Lucy explained briefly about the job and that it would mean a move to London if she was lucky enough to get it.

"I'd be a bit wary if I were you about going down there. Strange people in London you know."

"I think it would be good to have a real break and change of lifestyle."

"Oh well, good luck anyway and let me know how you get on. Don't forget to pay us a visit sometime soon. Talk things over. It's always good to discuss matters with someone. Helps to crystallise the mind."

"Thank you. I'll probably take you up on that."

Lucy bought herself a new black-and-white herringbone coat and black shoes for the occasion. The day of her interview arrived. She donned her new outfit and paraded in front of the mirror, turning first one way and then the other. She re-positioned a few loose strands of hair. She was pleased with her appearance and hoped she would not look too dishevelled at the end of her journey.

Lucy arrived at Waterloo station where she looked anxiously around in the bustling crowd for someone bearing a placard for the Agency. She eventually spotted the two people she had to meet and, as she walked towards them, they recognised Lucy from her description.

"Good morning. Lucy Barber I believe," said the gentleman as he shook Lucy firmly by the hand.

"Yes," she replied quickly eyeing him up and down.

He was of medium height, stocky build and sported a Jimmy Edward moustache. Lucy did not care for the look of him but then she remembered the old adage her mother had taught her, 'Never judge a book by its cover.' He was accompanied by an elegant, well-spoken lady whom she guessed would be about forty years old.

"Michael Evans," he said, "and this is my business partner Gladys Jones."

"Did you have a good journey?" enquired Gladys Jones.

"Yes thank you, very comfortable, and uneventful."

Lucy clutched her handbag as though it would give her some much-needed confidence. She smiled, doing her best to conceal her apprehension.

"I expect you could do with some refreshment, so we'll take a cab to the office. It'll be easier than the tube and you can get a drink when we arrive."

This seemed like a big adventure but as they approached the headquarters by a long, cobbled alleyway and climbed the steep, dark staircase to the second floor, Lucy felt the slender thread of confidence that she had mustered begin to slip. Perhaps this was not for her and maybe she should have listened to Mary. Nevertheless, she managed to get a grip of herself, pushing doubts into the back of her mind, and decided to do her best as always. After all it was not the end of the world if she was not accepted.

When they reached what passed for an office Lucy was asked

to sit and wait. The office reception area was dimly lit by a tiny skylight window and sparsely furnished with plastic stacking chairs. In the centre of the room, on a small coffee table marked with a number of white stains, was a large glass ashtray filled with stub ends of cigarettes. A young girl appeared, wearing a very short skirt, and finely balanced on stiletto heeled shoes.

"Would you like a cup of coffee?" she asked in a distinct cockney accent, to which Lucy said she would.

"Milk and sugar?"

"Just milk please."

With that, the girl tottered off wiggling her hips in her tight skirt.

As Lucy finished her coffee and placed the cup on the table, Michael Evans opened the inner door.

"Come through, Mrs Barber, please."

Lucy was asked to sit down and surprisingly there were only the two of them to interview. Lucy's past interviews had always been by a panel of at least four people. After asking some rather probing questions, Gladys Jones thanked Lucy and asked her to wait outside for a while. Michael Evans ushered her back to the waiting room where she nervously plucked at a tissue and awaited their decision. The lack of a window or air conditioning made the atmosphere stuffy, and the traffic noise was disconcerting to Lucy who was used to a quiet, semi-rural life.

Some time elapsed before the door was opened and a voice called,

"Come through, Mrs Barber."

Lucy returned to the office, fearing the worst but keeping her eyes fixed firmly on the two interviewers.

"We're sorry to tell you Mrs Barber that you haven't been successful at this stage. We both feel that it is an enormous step for you to take when you are obviously emotionally unsettled, but we will keep your name on our books for future reference. We are both of the opinion that although you are well suited to the job you should give yourself more time to settle in your mind that this change is right for you. It is a very big leap to make so quickly after such a traumatic time."

Lucy's heart sank. She wondered what she could have said

to give away her feelings so easily, or maybe, she consoled herself, it was just an excuse.

It was only as Lucy boarded the train to make the long journey home that the events of the day began to register in her somewhat turbulent mind. Not only did she feel disappointment but that feeling of failure began to rear its ugly head. Failure seemed to be her second name now and, although she had come to the conclusion that she did not really want the job, she would have liked the opportunity to turn it down. The train was quite full and as it pulled away from the platform a tall, slender fellow, with strawberry-blond hair and immaculately dressed walked towards the empty seat opposite Lucy.

"Do you mind if I sit here?"

"No please do."

Lucy fumbled in her bag for a book and aimlessly turned the pages having forgotten to insert a bookmark.

He pulled the Times newspaper from his leather briefcase, then tossed it effortlessly with his other luggage into the overhead rack and sat in the seat opposite Lucy.

"It's good to take the weight off my feet," he sighed. "It's been a busy old day."

Lucy lifted her face. From his appearance and his sartorial elegance, she deduced he must be a businessman. This was in stark contrast to a much older looking guy in the adjacent seat who she had carefully avoided and who she thought looked very bohemian to say the least, with his Jesus sandals, unkempt hair and straggling beard. The front of his hair, which he had a habit of tossing from his eyes, was tinged with a yellowish brown. This indicated he was a heavy smoker. One of the New Age travellers, she thought, and possibly an artist judging by his portfolio of paintings propped on the seat which he held lovingly as though it were a child. He kept giving her sideways glances. She tried to avert her eyes but found his glances compelling.

After putting on his spectacles, the well-scrubbed passenger opposite turned to the cryptic crossword. Lucy peeped over the top of her book and was amazed at the ease with which he filled the squares.

"Hmm, clever," she thought. As the train sped along, she put her book down and gazed out of the window watching the buildings of the city gradually recede to give way to the open countryside. She was soon reliving the events of the day which had certainly been a roller coaster, but the journey would give her time to settle and come to terms with her disappointment. She must after all put it in perspective.

Crossword complete, the gentleman in the opposite seat looked up. Lucy had felt his eyes on her over the top of his paper.

"Having a difficult time?" he asked as he placed his glasses into their case and snapped the lid shut. Tell me to mind my own business if you like."

"Why do you ask?"

"Well, the eyes give you away, you have been staring so disconsolately out of the window into faraway places. By the way they call me Sandy."

He smiled.

Gazing out of the window, Lucy realised, was a trait from childhood when she had wild and fantastic dreams. It usually happened when she found the lesson particularly boring and would be woken with a jolt when the teacher asked her a question knowing that she had not been listening and had no idea what had been discussed.

"Lucy, give me the date of the War of the Roses."

Lucy would stutter trying to think of an answer.

"Just as I thought you have no idea. Find out and write it a hundred times in addition to your homework."

Lucy had cornflower blue eyes and knew only too well that they did give away her emotions. Today she was not having wild fantasies but was wondering now she had her freedom whether it was really what she wanted. She remembered how elated she felt the day she had tripped down the steps from the court after being granted a Decree Nisi. Then she was free, free to do whatever she pleased. But it was short-lived once reality had set in.

"Oh, I'm Lucy. I've been for an interview but wasn't successful."

Sandy felt there was more to it than that but decided not to press her. After all it was none of his business. He did notice that she was not wearing a wedding ring as she fiddled with a plain gold band on her right hand.

"Never mind there'll be other opportunities, I'm sure. I'm going to the refreshment bar. I didn't get any lunch today. Would you like me to bring you something?" asked Sandy.

"I'd love a coffee, please."

Sandy returned after jostling his way down the centre of the train.

"Why is it the buffet bar always seems to be at the far end of the train?" he said as he placed two polystyrene mugs of coffee, a selection of sandwiches, cakes and chocolate on the centre table.

"Do help yourself."

"That's very kind of you."

Lucy tucked into a sandwich.

"How's your sandwich?"

"It's delicious and has just about hit the spot. I didn't realise how hungry I was until I started to eat. I feel better already," answered Lucy her spirits lifting a little.

During the course of their conversation, Lucy told Sandy where she lived. Sandy told Lucy that he lived in the Dales and that he was the director of a large company. This meant that he had quite a lot of travelling to do. Therefore, he was away from home for long periods. Today he was just returning from a trip to the Middle East where he was selling some of the components made in their factory. He also travelled all over Europe. It sounded plausible. It was not long before Lucy disclosed her recent situation.

"I thought there was more to it than being unsuccessful in an interview," he answered with empathy in his voice.

They were not far from their destination now and Lucy thought the journey had passed very quickly but was a little sorry that it was nearly over. She felt quite drawn towards Sandy. She guessed, though, it would probably be the last she would see of him. He had been good listener. Darkness was beginning to fall by the time the train reached the station and disgorged its passengers on to the dreary platform. After carefully gathering his paintings the 'Bohemian' stood to one side to allow Lucy to alight first while Sandy grabbed his luggage from the rack. Why was it that after disembarking a train everyone seemed to surge forward en masse rushing as though they had not a minute to spare? Bodies in this shapeless crowd craned their necks peering for a relative, friend or lover, hoping to be reunited perhaps after a period of separation and awaiting that fond embrace. Lucy felt a pang in her heart and a deep sinking feeling in the bottom of her stomach because there would not be anyone to meet her this time.

"This is it then. It was nice talking to you, Lucy," said Sandy as he began to make his way from the station and held out his hand.

As Lucy shook his hand, she detected a little squeeze that was slightly more than the usual handshake.

"Take care," and with that he was gone.

Lucy hailed a taxi. She was far too weary to get a bus. In twenty minutes, they reached her house. She paid for the taxi and ran up the steps to the front door. She delved in her handbag for the key that lurked somewhere in the bottom. She unlocked the door and when she entered the hallway that feeling of emptiness became even more acute. The place was wrapped in silence. How was she going to bear it?

"Oh well, I'll just have to get used to it," she said to herself as she kicked off her shoes and made towards the drinks cupboard. A stiff gin and tonic was the answer to erase the disappointment she had experienced. She curled up on the sofa to ease her aching feet and to ponder the events of the day. She was really too tired now to think about her next course of action, but her mind kept wandering to the two characters that she had encountered on her return journey. The 'Bohemian' was so different from anyone else that she knew and although they had not conversed, his expression was interesting. She felt that under the unconventional appearance lurked a sensitive character, but she also detected something a little sinister in some of the sideways glances he periodically gave her. Sandy was the opposite, and perhaps not so interesting, but a person who embodied the characteristics that her late mother would have found very acceptable.

Chapter 4

The days seemed to pass very slowly for Lucy. Each one commenced in the same way, scanning all the newspapers for jobs and so far without any luck. Her money was dwindling, and she was desperate to find employment. As a last resort she decided to apply for a job as a waitress at a new restaurant that was to open shortly. This was not what she was hoping for, but it would be a complete change. With a regular wage and tips, it should yield enough income as a temporary measure. A week after she had submitted her application she was called for an interview. The memory of the last one was all too fresh in her mind and it was with some apprehension that she went along.

She was greeted at the door by the concierge.

"Mrs Barber?" he asked in a very pleasant voice.

"That's right," replied Lucy, immediately at ease.

"Do come this way."

He showed her to a large waiting room at the end of a passage. There were sounds of laughter and giggles mingled with the clash of pans and crockery. They were obviously somewhere near the kitchens. It sounded like a very happy working environment, in stark contrast to the London agency, she thought, as she was directed to a large armchair.

"Please have a seat. Mrs Hamilton won't be long."

Lucy wondered whether she would be able to get out of it as she sank into the plush cushions. It all appeared rather grand for waitressing work.

The door opened and an elegant lady with an up-to-the-minute coiffure came towards her,

"Come through to the office and take a seat."

Lucy walked boldly through and since there was no one else present she assumed the lady was Mrs Hamilton. She was surprised that the lady sat next to her rather than at the desk, so she was instantly placed at ease.

"Now, Mrs Barber, would you like to tell me why you have applied to do waitressing? Judging by your application you seem to be overqualified for this kind of work."

Lucy explained her circumstances in as few details as possible. She said that it was to be a temporary solution for her, but she envisaged staying for at least a year and maybe longer depending on how her present situation worked out. That satisfied Mrs Hamilton who went on to explain that they did put a great deal of time and effort into training their staff and that she was looking for a commitment of at least a year. She continued with a few more questions skilfully eliciting as much information as possible and concluded,

"We employ staff initially on a three-month trial period to see if they are suitable and, most importantly, whether they feel able to fit in. On that basis I am willing to offer you the job."

Lucy replied without hesitation, "Thank you Mrs Hamilton. I'd like to accept it and I'll do my very best for you."

"As you are probably aware, this is a new restaurant which we're not opening for another two months or so but we're recruiting staff in readiness. During this time, we'll be having some short training sessions for new staff which we would like you to attend. We'll contact you in due course to formalise your appointment."

Lucy shook hands and took her leave. She was over the moon as she left the building. It felt as though she was walking on air. She was so excited. This was the first positive news she had received for a long time. As soon as she arrived home, she picked up the phone,

"Hello Mary. Lucy here."

"Oh hello. Good to hear your voice. I was thinking about you the other day and wondered how you fared in London."

"Oh, not well but since returning I've secured a job as a waitress at the new restaurant opening in the White Horse, starting in about two months, depending on when the refurbishment is complete."

"Jolly well done. Why don't you come up for a few days? Malc's away for a week and it'll be a good opportunity to catch up on all that's been happening."

"Thank you. That sounds like a wonderful idea."

"Why don't you come up tomorrow. Can you make it in time for lunch?"

Lucy arrived at Three Chimneys the next day, as planned, in time for lunch. As she pulled up at the top of the drive, she was met by Mary accompanied by Buster their big black Labrador wagging his tail, which was his seal of approval. He ran around her, his tail swishing from side to side. He licked her hands as if they were old buddies.

"Hello, and welcome to 'Three Chimneys'," Mary said as she welcomed Lucy with open arms. "How good to see you. Are you sure you've not come for six months," she went on in a jocular fashion, glancing at all the luggage, as she gave Lucy an affectionate hug.

"Oh well, you know me. I always did bring everything but the kitchen sink."

"Come in and I'll show you to your room. You can have a wash and brush up and then we'll eat. How does that sound?"

"A very good idea."

Mary had prepared a scrumptious-looking cold buffet which they enjoyed, washed down with a bottle of white wine, sitting in the new sun lounge. Malcolm had always kept a good wine cellar, Lucy remembered. They chatted for a long time about family and friends and of course the subject of her divorce came up.

Lucy also told Mary all about her trip to London.

"I know you're disappointed you didn't get the job at the agency, but I must agree with their judgement. It would have been too big a step to take at present which you would probably have regretted later. Somehow, from what you have told me, it just didn't seem right for you."

"Oh well, it's probably for the best. In fact, I've been coming to that conclusion myself. Anyway, I've put it behind me now. The job I have lined up doesn't sound very challenging, but you never know. I could become manageress!" Lucy tossed her head, laughed and, cupping her glass of wine, ventured,

"Coming back on the train I met this very pleasant chap. He sat opposite me, bought me coffee and sandwiches. Apparently, he and his wife don't spend much time together because he is away from home so much. She stays for long periods with her parents. He claimed his marriage is really over, but they haven't done anything about it formally."

"You haven't heard the other side of the story," Mary replied, "and remember what I said to you before you went. Beware!"

"Well, I don't suppose I'll ever see him again, but I can't get him off my mind."

Lucy continued:

"There was another fellow who looked rather like a New Age Traveller. Bohemian. Judging by the care he took of a large portfolio of paintings propped up on the seat, I would say he was an artist and his appearance was in keeping."

"These two men are certainly absorbing your mind at the moment but do remember what I said. Would you like a refill?"

"Thank you. I would, please."

Mary poured the wine and sat thoughtfully.

"Do you remember that medical student? Patrick, I think was his name. You were infatuated with him,"

"I certainly do. That wasn't infatuation. It was real love, first love and nothing has ever matched it."

"Then there were the two Americans who took us rowing. One of them owned a Buick. They arranged another date but didn't turn up, rotters! I guess they weren't impressed. We hitch-hiked everywhere."

"Those were the days, no money, carefree and nothing but romance."

"I'm of the opinion that those experiences have a lasting effect and never really leave you. What do you think?"

"I'm sure you're right."

"Buster's getting restless and looking for his lead. He's ready for his walk. Come on Buster lets go to the beach," Mary said as she patted his head.

The Northumberland sand was almost silver and very fine. Buster loved racing back and forth for his ball and a stick that they had acquired along the way. It was a sunny day, but they could feel a chill wind on their faces. In the distance they could see Bamburgh Castle.

"Perhaps you would like to spend tomorrow in Alnwick, Lucy?"

"Yes, that would be interesting."

After a week of walking, eating and talking it was time for Lucy to make her way home.

***

Sandy's chance encounter on the train with Lucy had made him restless. He became conscious that he was thinking more and more about her. He would love to take her out but realised that, if he went out with Lucy, it could spell trouble if he were ever discovered. Nevertheless, he decided his feelings were strong enough to warrant the risk. Surely, there could be no harm in meeting her to go to the cinema or, perhaps, a drink for companionship. After all he and Helen, to all intents and purposes, were separated. Helen seemed to be quite happy living most of the time with her parents. They were both aged and infirm and happy with her support. Helen showed no interest in travelling with him and apart from the odd short visit he made to her parents, they never saw one another. When Sandy was not travelling he lived in their house alone. He took advantage of this situation by participating in sporting activities. When not travelling, he spent most weekends on the golf course. He found this relaxing and a good distraction from the pressure of work. Sandy remembered where Lucy had said she lived, so the next time he was passing through he would pay her visit. After all, the worst that could happen was that she would turn him away.

He opened the little wrought iron gate and walked up the path, with its neat borders on each side, and gave the brass door knocker a good bang, but there was no reply. Sandy was unsure whether to be pleased or sad. However, he sat in his car for a little while before he plucked up enough courage to leave a hastily written note with his telephone number.

The journey home from Northumberland was uneventful, but Lucy was mindful, yet again, that she had to return to an empty house. She wondered whether she would ever become used to it. As she opened the door, she could see the postman had been. There were one or two personal letters along with a good deal of junk mail. There was a letter with an Australian postmark, obviously from Richard, but then another unstamped envelope, with unfamiliar writing, caught her eye. She tore it open and was most agreeably surprised to find a short note from Sandy. It read, 'Was in the area so called but no one answered so I guess you were out. This is my telephone number if you feel like getting in touch. Maybe we could meet for a drink. Hope you don't think me presumptuous.'

She was not surprised to find herself feeling quite excited at the thought of meeting Sandy again. She remembered the extra squeeze he had given her hand when they said goodbye at the railway station. He had painted a sad picture of his marriage so she supposed there could be little harm in meeting for a drink, but Mary's warning was ringing loud and clear in her ears. Sandy had left the ball in her court. Her heart was telling her one thing but common sense another. Her emotions finally overcame common sense and she responded to the note.

Lucy's hand was shaking when she picked up the phone. A young sounding voice answered.

"Oh yes, Mrs Barber, I'll get him for you."

"Tell her I'm busy at the moment. Take a number and I'll call her back."

'Another one,' thought Mandy, his secretary, who was quite used to this ritual. Sandy now had a note of her number. A canny ploy.

About five minutes later Lucy's phone rang.

"Sandy here."

"Oh hello. I wasn't expecting you to ring so quickly."

"Hope you didn't mind me calling round the other day."

"Well, it was somewhat of a surprise but of course not. I'd been to stay with a friend in Northumberland for a few days and must have just missed you."

"The Northumberland coast is spectacular. I've been a few times. I was wondering whether you would care to meet me for a drink sometime?"

"I'd love to," replied Lucy trying not to sound too eager.

"How about seven thirty at The Crown then?"

"That sounds fine."

"OK then I'll see you there." With that, Sandy hung up.

Lucy parked her car and walked animatedly towards the entrance. She found Sandy already inside and waiting. As she expected, he was well turned out in smart casual dress. She could not help but notice his rather expensive looking brogues. They passed the evening talking about their lives and loves and seemed to get on well. She was blown away with Sandy. He was very attentive and talked with ease about many topics. He said he was a keen golf player and also liked a game of tennis. He had an engaging smile which exposed a set of brilliant white teeth. He was a charming person. They met a few times, usually going for a walk and then calling at the local for a drink or occasionally going to the cinema. One such evening, when they had been walking on the common deep in conversation, they had not noticed the black clouds gathering overhead. A very heavy storm was suddenly upon them. By the time they had reached Lucy's house they were drenched and uncomfortably wet. Neither of them was prepared for such an eventuality.

"We look like two drowned rats," said Lucy laughingly.

Sandy saw the funny side and had a good laugh too.

"Would you like to come in for a cup of coffee and get dried off before going home?"

"I'll certainly take you up on that offer. My clothes are so wet they are sticking to me."

Lucy dashed upstairs and returned with a dressing gown that Richard had left behind and a bath towel.

"Here," she said handing them to Sandy, "You had better go to the bathroom and dry yourself. Bring down your wet clothes and I'll dry them for you."

She showered and had a change of clothes then went into the kitchen to prepare the coffee. Sandy followed.

"Let me carry the tray for you."

He carried the tray into the sitting room and sat next to her on the sofa. Lucy's heart was pounding. She could hardly contain her excitement and passion that the close proximity of his body aroused in her. Her hand trembled as she poured the coffee almost spilling it. She had only just replaced her cup in its saucer when Sandy nudged a little closer to her and she could feel his hands caressing her hair. She turned her head and their eyes met. He pulled her closer to him and were soon locked in a passionate embrace. Her heart beat rapidly as she felt his fingers undoing the buttons on her blouse. Her breasts exposed she could feel the softness of his lips as he kissed them tenderly. He pulled her into her bedroom.

"The same eyes that appealed so much to me on the train, full of melancholy, so sad. Tell me, what are they hiding?" Sandy whispered as he eased himself alongside her.

Lucy felt the warmth exuding from him as their now naked bodies became entwined. She felt the steady beat of his heart gradually increase as she rested her head on his firm muscular, chest. His gentleness was soon eclipsed by sheer passion. He turned and flung himself on top of her. She wrapped her legs around his sinewy form, neither capable of, nor desiring, to resist. It was a magical experience and neither wanted to break the magic, as they lay locked in one another's arms, beautifully exhausted.

Looking at his watch, Sandy eventually broke the spell saying, "I have to leave because I've an early appointment at the office and must go home to change first."

He dressed and tidied his hair and with a swift kiss left Lucy feeling rather saddened and bemused. It all seemed so casual and mundane now, almost of the moment. Nevertheless, this night was the first of many. Sandy and Lucy began to spend longer and longer in each other's company and sometimes Sandy would stay the weekend. Their relationship gradually developed, or so Lucy thought, even though they always met at her house which she never questioned.

"I do love you so much," Sandy would say, holding her tightly every time they met.

Freeing herself from his embrace Lucy said on more than one occasion,

"Well, if you love me so much why can't we get together on a permanent basis?"

"Soon," was always the reply but it never progressed.

Sandy knew that Helen would never divorce him because her financial situation was secure while they remained together. He knew this was important to Helen because she liked the luxuries a good income afforded. He was happy to continue in this way. Although he loved Lucy, he did not wish to make the break to move in with her, after all he had the best of both worlds, a comfortable home and a loving relationship without the responsibility. Perhaps it was a little selfish he thought to himself. He told Lucy he needed time to sort things out because Helen was being particularly difficult. She neither wanted to be with him nor did she want anyone else to take her place.

"That's a very selfish attitude and it makes me feel very uneasy. I'm not happy about allowing the situation to drift any longer. A decision must be made."

***

"Helen dear, I've been thinking" said her mother over a cup of coffee one morning, as tactfully as possible, "please don't take this the wrong way, but don't you think you should go home for a while. I'm sure Sandy is missing you. You're spending less and less time together. I think you should go home before it's too late. You've been with us a long time now," Helen's mother continued. "Is something wrong between you? Sandy's weekend visits are becoming less frequent and when he is here there seems to be a tension between you. You've certainly been a great help to us both and we'll miss you, but that's not the point. It seems to me that your marriage is at stake. Are you sure Sandy isn't seeing someone else?"

Helen did not take kindly to parental interference. Nevertheless, she had to concede that her mother was probably right. They had not approved of her marriage in the first place. They thought that Sandy was somewhat of a Lothario. There had been many rumours about him at the time, but Helen had been madly in love with Sandy and would not listen to anyone. She was so certain that this time he really did love her and she would be able to keep him. Recently though, Helen noticed that when she telephoned he was never at home. When she rang the office he was always at a meeting or away on business. The usual excuses. She began to suspect that there might be another woman involved despite not wanting to believe it. However cool she felt towards him, she was not going to let anyone else take her place.

A few days later Helen told her parents that she had decided to go home for a week or so but that she would return before long.

"I'm pleased to hear that. Mrs. Walker will always come in to give us a hand whenever we need it, so you've no need to worry."

Helen packed some clothes and left within a couple of days. When she arrived home late one afternoon she found the house locked up and, on ringing the office, was told Sandy was at a meeting. The hours ticked by and still no sign of him. Helen, who by now was tired and curious as to her husband's whereabouts decided the best thing to do was to try to get some sleep. As she was plumping the cushions and tidying up, before going upstairs, she heard the turn of a key in the lock.

"Hello! What's brought you home? Something up?" called Sandy, somewhat surprised to find the house lit up and wondering why Helen had come home without telling him. He stepped through the door and immediately went to the bathroom to remove any tell-tale signs of his extra-marital affair.

"You're working late tonight," called Helen mustering a sarcastic tone.

"Had to go to a meeting in preparation for the convention in Paris next week."

"Paris? You haven't told me anything about going to Paris."

Sandy slowly made his way down the stairs.

"Why didn't you tell me you were coming home?"

"Thought it would be a nice surprise for you. A trip to Paris sounds exciting. I think I'd like to come with you. I could do a bit of shopping and sight-seeing."

Sandy's heart dropped into his boots. He was in a fix. What was he going to tell Lucy?

"I've changed my mind about things and think we should try to keep our marriage alive with a bit more conviction, so I decided to make a start and how better than to go to Paris together."

Sandy went to pour himself a drink.

"Would you like a drink, Helen?"

"I'd rather have a kiss."

With drink in hand Sandy bent down and gave Helen a peck on her cheek.

"Well, that's better than nothing I suppose. That's some rather special after shave you're wearing for an office meeting," she taunted recognising the expensive Chanel perfume lingering on his jacket.

Sandy was taken aback for a minute but tried to brush the comment aside and said,

"Well, what about this trip to Paris, then? I was planning to leave on Friday morning, driving down to London and taking an afternoon flight. Are you sure you'll be feeling up to it after your long journey back today?"

"I'll be fine. There's time for me to recover."

When Sandy arrived at the office the next day, he had to legitimise his trip to Paris by arranging to meet a couple of business associates. He thought Helen was more than a little suspicious of his movements. He then had to explain his new arrangement to Lucy. He could have done without all this hassle. He scratched his head and, pushing back his hair, picked up the phone.

"Hello, Lucy. I hope you won't be too disappointed, but I have to go to London on urgent business and will have to call off our trip to Paris." Careful not to mention Helen's return, "We'll organise it for a later date. I'll contact you sometime from London. In any case I'll ring you when I get home."

"What a shame. Never mind we'll have it to look forward to." Lucy's voice conveyed her disappointment.

"Goodbye and take care. Love you." Sandy hung up.

Lucy thought that this was the kind of situation that would eventually put a strain on any marriage and maybe this is what Helen had endured over the years. She now had to fill the weekend which would inevitably drag, especially as she would be anxiously awaiting a phone call.

Monday morning came but still no phone call. Lucy could contain herself no longer, so she decided to ring the office.

"May I speak to Mr. Thomas? she asked his secretary."

"I'm afraid Mr. Thomas is in Paris and won't be back until later."

"Oh, thank you," stammered Lucy.

She was flabbergasted and hastily rang off before she started to cry. So he had lied to her. This was unforgivable. She wandered in a daze with Mary's remark, 'beware', ringing in her ears. Surely he could not have lied to her. There must be an explanation. Sandy rang the next day giving what sounded like a plausible explanation but deep in her heart she knew that it was not the truth especially as he was going to be busy for the next few weeks. She felt raw inside and let down.

By this time Lucy, had commenced her new job as a waitress at the newly opened restaurant. The management staff were particularly pleased with the way in which she approached her work. She was a good timekeeper and efficient. She looked after regular and casual clients alike receiving quite a lot of money in tips. Mrs. Hamilton had called her to the office one morning to tell her.

"We've have had a number of compliments about you, Lucy, so I think it is only fair that they should be passed on to you. Keep up the good work and you'll be in line for promotion."

Lucy was overwhelmed.

"Thank you so much," was all she could manage.

She heard from Sandy a few times, and saw him occasionally, but she sensed a cooling off in their relationship, and when they were together things were not quite the same. Lucy was careful to keep her suspicions to herself, but she was aware that she was letting herself down because any self-respecting person would have broken the ties, but she could not bear to be without him and, ever the romantic, continued to hope that everything would work out in the end.

Sandy and Helen jogged along for a few weeks.

"By the way, in case you have forgotten it's our wedding anniversary tomorrow, so I've taken the liberty of booking a table for us at the 'White Horse'.

"That's some way to go for a meal. Can't you find something a bit closer to home?" he answered. He remembered that was where Lucy had started to work. He was unsure of her shifts. It was the last thing he wanted to celebrate.

"Your enthusiasm knows no bounds. I've heard very good reports of the place. The restaurant has only recently opened I understand. Anyway, it's too late to cancel now."

Sandy had to accept the situation and hope that Lucy would not be working. He felt apprehensive, though.

Helen made a special effort indulging in a hairdo and a manicure. She also wore an outfit that she knew Sandy liked. He came home from the office early and presented her with a beautiful bouquet of her favourite flowers. It all seemed quite contrived but nevertheless, they went along with the pretence. They ordered a drink from the bar and were given a menu.

"Good choice."

"Rather expensive though."

"Don't worry, have whatever you'd like, Helen. It is a special occasion."

Poor Lucy's mouth dropped open when she came through to take the orders.

"Sandy, what a surprise," she exclaimed.

"Oh, hello Lucy," said Sandy, "This is my wife, Helen. We're celebrating our wedding anniversary," he answered with his usual aplomb.

Now she knew the truth but managed to gain control. She would not let Sandy know how upset this chance encounter had made her feel and proceeded to take their order.

"Who's that?" asked Helen "Whoever it is she knows you well enough to call you by your first name."

"Oh, just someone I met on the train when I was returning from a meeting in London. She confided that she had just been declined for a job and was feeling rather low at the time. I see her about sometimes."

Helen raised an eyebrow, "I see."

Despite her misgivings about Sandy, Lucy was still shocked to see him with his wife. She wanted to shout at him to let everyone know what he had done and what a cad he was but something from within instantly prevented her. Remembering her recent meeting with Mrs. Hamilton, she took their order in a very polite and dignified fashion, held her head high and walked to the kitchen. After presenting the chef with the order she rushed to the staff room for a few minutes in which to compose herself. There was no way she would allow anyone to know how upset she was feeling. She sensed that under that casual exterior Sandy must be feeling very embarrassed and uncomfortable. 'It serves him right,' she thought.

Sandy and Helen continued with their meal, but it took all Lucy's will power not to drop the food in his lap. Much to her relief they made their visit as brief as possible. The tension between them was palpable.

"That was a quick meal for an anniversary celebration," one of her colleagues remarked.

"I think his wife must not be feeling too well," she sniggered.

Lucy struggled through the rest of her shift almost in a daze but acutely aware that she must not make any blunders.

The next morning, while Lucy was drinking her mid-morning coffee, the telephone rang. She let it ring for a while, guessing it would be Sandy but then could not resist the temptation.

It was indeed Sandy who said, in a very contrite manner, "I'm ringing, Lucy, to say how sorry I am that you were placed in such an embarrassing situation. Let me try to explain."

"It doesn't need much explaining," Lucy answered with bitterness in her voice.

"Look, Lucy, it's not like you think it is. Just give me a little time to work things out. I do love you more than anyone else. You know that."

"Funny way of showing it then. I think you need to sort yourself out. Anyway, I don't want to see you again because I can't trust you."

"Oh well, if that's how you feel then I guess it's goodbye." With that Sandy put down the phone.

Chapter 5

Lucy was distraught. Another disappointment. She felt hurt and let down but was determined to hold on to her self-respect. She would take advantage of the warm sunshine and go for a walk along the river with a book. Perhaps that would distract her from her misery. She knew she must not become too immersed in herself. After all, she shared the guilt. She had known Sandy was a married man. A few days away would help to assuage the pain but this was the wrong time to be asking for time off at The White Horse. On her way to the river Lucy called in at the library to change her book. She would try to find a humorous novel. After all, laughter is the best medicine, although she would find it hard to raise a laugh at present.

Lucy was a regular at the library. "Ah, good morning Mrs Barber. Your book's in. Would you like to take it?" asked the librarian humming a little tune as he delved into the bookcase of books waiting to be collected. Jo was Lucy's favourite assistant, with his spectacles perched on the end of his nose and a cheery personality. He was just the kind of person she needed today to give her spirits a boost.

"Yes please. I was looking for a good read, Jo."

"Oh well, you'll enjoy this one then," he said with a big smile on his face, handing her the book.

Lucy walked across the park and through the little wicket gate which took her to the path alongside the river. The willows draped their large fronds over the water's edge and the ducks played hide-and-seek among them. She walked on until she eventually came to a seat where she sat and watched the river life. A duck glided down the river, followed by a retinue of ducklings striving to keep up with their mother; moor hens too, with their red and yellow tipped beaks, were running into the water and frantically twitching their tails as they paddled. Lucy opened her book, leafed quickly through the pages then read the biography of the author. She started to read the first chapter but thoughts of Sandy began to drift through the words. She could not concentrate so decided to eat the snack and drink that she had purchased on leaving the library. After she had finished, she threw the crusts and last few crumbs to the ducks. They all swam and sculled quickly over the water, each scrabbling for a morsel but were outdone by greedy gulls swooping down to steal the prize. She decided to walk further along the riverside walk. She had never been this far before and was quite surprised to come across a vast pastureland with cows on the opposite side lazily chewing the cud and occasionally creeping towards the edge of the bank to take a long draught of the cool water. One black and white cow lifted her head and seemed to blink a sad brown eye, as much as to say, 'who are you?'

In the distance she could see a few people. From her stance it looked as though they might be fishermen but as she drew closer, and they came properly into focus, she discerned two artists with their easels, obviously painting the riverside scene. The artist furthest away from her, with his straggling beard and long hair, was instantly recognisable as the 'artistic one' she had briefly encountered on the train when returning from her disappointing interview. He looked up as she drew closer to him and, recognising her, said in an unexpectedly refined voice,

"What a surprise. Fancy seeing you here."

Smiling Lucy replied, "Just out for a walk to enjoy the sunshine. I was right then. I thought you were an artist when I saw you on the train."

"I dabble a bit, you know. It's particularly enjoyable down here on a sunny day like today. It's a good way of keeping one's thoughts occupied because you really do become immersed in the experience."

He put down his brushes and, stepping away from his easel, suggested they should take a seat on a nearby bench.

"I could do with a break."

"I envy painters so much. It must be wonderful to encapsulate a magical scene with a palette of beautiful colours and what appears to be a few casual brush strokes. When I was at school I longed to be able to paint but showed no aptitude for it. I remember my pathetic attempts at trying to paint when a vase of flowers or some other object was placed in front of the class and we were told to paint what we actually saw. My work never bore any resemblance to what I was seeing."

"It's surprising how many people are discouraged from painting by bad school experiences. You must've been one of the unlucky ones. By the way, I'm Philip. Pip for short."

"I'm Lucy. May I call you Pip then?"

"Sure."

They chatted for a while and it gradually became apparent that Pip was a well-known local artist.

"I've seen your paintings hanging in some of the local galleries but of course I didn't realise that artist was you. The penny's just dropped."

"I give lessons at the local art college and I'll willingly give you some help to get started if you are really interested."

Lucy thought for a moment and decided that this would make a good diversion.

"I'd like that very much."

He turned to Lucy and raised his eyebrow as he spoke, "Painting's very therapeutic you know."

Lucy went home with a much lighter spring to her step and found a letter from her son awaiting her. Richard was coming home for a short while to visit the parent company and would she put up with him for a few days. Lucy telephoned immediately, hardly able to contain her excitement at the thought of seeing Richard if only for a short while.

"Wonderful news and of course you know you'll be welcome. I've so much to tell you."

They did not linger on the phone, but Richard did tell her that he had a new girlfriend called Sophie. And that she was a stunner. He would tell her all about their meeting in his next letter when he would contact her with confirmation of dates and flight times once they had been finalised.

Pip was at their prearranged meeting place as promised, equipped with a spare easel, set of paint brushes, water colours and paper. Lucy was both apprehensive and excited as Pip greeted her.

"Hi there, Lucy. Lovely day for painting although I do sometimes like the greyer days with cloud. It can be more atmospheric and adds another interesting dimension to the painting. After all life isn't always sunny," he chuckled.

Lucy, expecting to get covered in paint, protected her clothes with a large apron that she used for gardening.

"These'll come in handy," she said thrusting her hands into its large pockets.

"You certainly look the part."

Pip started by showing Lucy how to hold and control her brush.

"Try writing and doodling to start with. In that way you'll become used to holding a paint brush."

After a while Pip who had been keeping an eye on Lucy over his shoulder said,

"You seem to be doing quite well. I suggest we move on to the next step which is to lay a flat-water wash. For this you'll need to select and mix colours."

It all sounded rather technical to Lucy. However she persevered but just as she thought she was beginning to get the hang of things she felt paint trickling down her hand.

"I can't stop the paint from running down the brush," she cried in exasperation.

"Calm down, just change the angle of the brush like so," Pip demonstrated.

"Oh!" exclaimed Lucy, as she copied Pip's movements, "it works!"

They continued to meet several times a week during which time Lucy made good progress and amazed herself.

The letter from Richard arrived a few weeks later telling his mother that he would be arriving at the end of the week which did not give her a great deal of time for preparation. She explained to Pip that she would have to forgo the painting sessions for a couple of weeks while her son was home. Lucy was disappointed about this, but it was a small price to pay for seeing Richard. She was so excited. She had missed him a lot, but it was due in part to her encouragement that he landed this posting. At the same time, she was thrilled for him, although she knew she would not see him regularly or even at all, so this visit really was a bonus.

It was good to have family around and it certainly took her

mind off all the latest events. Lucy had prepared his favourite meal of steak and kidney pie accompanied by a good bottle of red wine.

"No one makes steak and kidney pie like you Mum," Richard flattered his mother.

She glowed with pride as a result of Richard's obvious pleasure and the effect of half a bottle of wine, something she was not used to now. They sat well into the night talking about all the events that had taken place since his leaving.

"I suppose you are aware that father's on his own again?" asked Richard.

"As a matter of fact he did let me know. He wrote to me and it does seem as though he wants to be, what shall I say, a little more friendly. The divorce was all so hastily managed in the first place."

"I guess so," replied Richard "but that's all in the past now and it's best not to dwell on it," he went on diplomatically. "Anyway, the good news is that Sophie and I have been seeing one another for some weeks now. She's Irish. You'll love her beautiful auburn hair and the Irish lilt in her voice. She's great fun. We do a lot of walking and also share an interest in music. She has an eclectic taste much like mine."

"Is it serious then Richard?"

"Yes, it's looking that way. I hope we'll get married but I haven't asked her yet."

"Why is she in Australia and how did you meet her?"

"Well, she graduated from medical school and went to Australia to gain some experience before finally deciding in which branch of medicine to specialise. We met quite by accident, literally, when I was taken to accident and emergency after falling and breaking my ankle while at work."

"What a lucky break, pardon the pun," laughed Lucy. "How come you didn't tell me you broke an ankle?"

"Didn't want to worry you. I know what you're like. Sophie lost her mother tragically, not long before she went to Australia. She continued with the arrangement because she said it's what her mother would've wanted. It must have been very painful for her."

“I’m pleased you share some interests. It makes a relationship so much easier if you do things together.”

“Well, we both work very tight schedules, but we enjoy weekends by the sea where we can swim and snorkel. We also like riding the waves when the weather’s right.”

“Quite a change of lifestyle for you Richard. I am surprised. She must have turned your head.”

“We both enjoy listening to classical music for a quieter time.”

“She sounds a charming girl but make sure she’s right for you. Don’t do anything too hasty, mind,” said Lucy thoughtfully as her own situation flashed through her mind. “Have you told your father yet?”

“No, I’d rather tell him in person when I go to see him. When you come for your holiday you’ll be able to meet Sophie.”

“Maybe in about six months’ time. That’ll give me something to look forward to.”

Richard looked up a few old school and university pals. He and his mother went here, there and everywhere eating out as much as they could afford. Lucy found that she could not indulge herself too often now. Sharing assets after divorce results in a change of lifestyle and status. Adaptation takes time. The two weeks passed quickly, and it was soon time for Richard to leave. Lucy drove him to the station to catch the train for King’s Cross. She had ambivalent feelings towards railway stations remembering the feeling of desolation when she arrived that day from London and there was no one to meet her. She too had experienced the joy and excitement of meeting Richard but she knew today would be more like the first time which would be accompanied by that sinking feeling his departure would bring and which she tried to push to the back of her mind. Lucy knew it would be a long time before she would see him again although they glibly talked of a holiday.

“Goodbye Richard, darling,” she managed as she felt a lump rise in her throat. “Have a safe journey. Don’t forget to give my love to Sophie. Tell her I’m looking forward to meeting her.” She stood waving and watching the train until it was out of sight then turned with tears in her eyes, wondering what she should do for the rest of the day, thinking perhaps she would walk down to the river to see if by any chance Pip was there. Maybe a bit of painting would calm her down.

As she approached the clearing, she could see one or two of the regular artists but Pip was nowhere to be seen. She felt quite disappointed about this, but she supposed he was not able to be there every day. She would try again the next day. Lucy walked home, wrote a birthday card for Mary and went to post it. By the time she returned home it was time to get ready for work.

"I saw that chap, who was in here the other day s'posed to be celebratin' his wedding anniversary, with another woman in town," were the words Lucy was greeted with by her colleague when she walked into the restaurant. Lucy did not wish to be reminded of Sandy, or at least so she thought, but at the very mention of his name she felt a rapid increase in her heartbeat. The chemistry between them was very strong. Why was she so attracted to him? Seemingly she was not alone. The thought of someone else with him sickened her even more. Perhaps she had been too hasty in dismissing him, but then she felt that she could never trust him again though she continued to try to find excuses for his behaviour. She was pretty sure in her mind that he was not happily married. She wondered why. They seemed to have everything going for them, although in the course of their conversations, Sandy had confided that they were not able to have children. This weighed heavily on him. He had always hoped that they would have a family but Helen did not appear to mind. Lucy deduced it had created considerable tension between them.

Lucy mused there is nothing straight forward in a relationship and no two are ever the same. Some couples appear on the surface to be blissfully happy with their lot but certainly no one knows what lurks beneath the surface. She was certain she would not have any more to do with Sandy... or would she? Would she be able to resist him if he approached her again?

"Penny for 'em," piped a voice from the other side of the room. "Don't say you are smitten with him too."

Lucy pulled herself up sharply. Her colleague was more intuitive than she had given her credit for. "Oh no, not a chance," she replied as she busied herself setting the tables for dinner.

She knew this was a lie as she carefully folded the brilliant white table napkins.

Pip seemed to have vanished. Lucy went down to the riverbank a few more days but he was nowhere to be seen. She plucked up courage to ask one of the other artists who was there most days if he had seen him.

"No. He packed up one evening and hasn't been down since," came the reply.

This appeared very strange but Lucy assumed there must be a good reason for it and sadly wended her way home. She was disappointed but more to the point she realised how much she had relied on his good nature over the past turbulent weeks. She found painting very restful and Pip was a good teacher. It certainly diverted her thoughts from Sandy but at least she could enrol at the college for the next class.

Lucy commenced the following week. She remembered that Pip said he taught at the local college, so she made some discreet enquiries about him and was told that he had taken compassionate leave. Apparently he had an elderly mother who had been taken very ill. He had to leave in a hurry because the prognosis was not good. Lucy was sad, aware of the distress he must be feeling but also not immune to the effect that it was having on her. There would be no more lessons on the riverbank. Somehow painting in the classroom was not quite the same.

Buoyed up a little by another letter from Richard to say he was working out some flight time and costs for her visit, Lucy's disappointment waned a little. He thought early bookings would be more favourable. A trip to Australia, how good that sounded. It was a country she had always desired to visit and it looked now as though it could become a reality.

On her way home from college the next afternoon who should she bump into but Sandy! At first she did not notice him on the other side of the road, but he had spotted her and crossed deliberately to encounter her. "Well, fancy meeting you of all people. Where have you been keeping yourself for the last few months?" Before Lucy could answer he asked, "D'you fancy a drink?" She could not resist. They went to a small wine bar where he thought they were unlikely to be recognised. "What would you like?"

"I'll have an orange juice, please."

Sandy ordered himself a lager and accompanied Lucy to a table in a cosy corner where they could chat without being overheard.

"Helen and I have had some terrible rows since that evening in the restaurant and she has returned to her parents, so I'm on my own again. She won't contemplate a divorce at any price, so we've reached stalemate. She says she's gone principally to look after her parents so technically she's not left me. Clever move." He spoke in subdued and remorseful tones.

"A difficult situation in which to find oneself. Not much you can do about it, I suppose."

"Will you have dinner with me tomorrow evening? It would brighten me up and maybe we could pick up where we left off."

Lucy knew this would be a retrograde step. "Look you're in a difficult situation at the moment and it would be foolish for me to allow you to complicate it further. So the answer is, no thank you."

Sandy felt his heart sink. Notwithstanding the blow to his ego, for the first time in his life, he felt that at last he had found a very special person; someone with whom he would love to spend the rest of his days. She was resisting his advances so where had he gone wrong?

"I knew when I first set eyes on you that day on the train that you were the one for me. I do love you, Lucy. Please give it some thought. Tonight, I am dining with my sister who has come to stay for a few days. We meet from time to time. Yesterday she dragged me around the shops; something I detest."

So that explained who he had been seen with in the town! She must not be too hasty to judge but nevertheless, she knew that she had made the correct decision.

Chapter 6

Lucy wandered aimlessly around the kitchen. She had not slept well and could not focus her thoughts this morning. She gazed out of the window hoping for inspiration, but nothing came to mind. It was a drizzly wet day so gardening was not an option. Marmalade the cat was on the windowsill. She stroked him and he began to purr.

"You know, Marmalade, I think a strong cup of coffee might help."

She sat drinking her coffee and thinking about past events when Marmalade made a sudden bound on to her lap causing her to spill her drink.

"There now, look what you've made me do."

"Meow."

As she mopped up the spillage she thought about her painting and Pip. She was becoming very good at it and some of her work was to be displayed at the college later on in the year. She had heard that Pip would be away indefinitely which made her sad. She missed his lessons and his encouragement. He was impeccably behaved and had never made any amorous advances towards her. Sandy continued to tug at her heart strings but she tried to put all thoughts of him out of her mind. She kept reminding herself that she still had her holiday in Australia to look forward to. This always cheered her.

The dark clouds hung uncertainly in the sky and the drizzle turned to heavy rain. The coffee gave her a little boost and Lucy decided it would be a good time to tidy some of her very cluttered drawers. She was an inveterate hoarder. She thought the big drawer in the pine dresser would be a good place to start. She began to remove its contents when tucked away in the back corner she found the old sweet tin again. She shook it, then removed the lid. It was full of old coins. As she sifted through them, one silver coin in particular caught her eye. It was an Irish threepence piece. She carefully removed it and placing it the palm of her hand allowed its memories to unlock themselves. Sweet memories that had been pushed into the back of her mind and lay dormant for many years and only fleetingly did she allow these memories to surface and find their way into her conscious thoughts. Oh, how cruel life can be.

Lucy's memory drifted back to the time when she was working on the plastic surgery unit as part of her general nursing training. This was situated in a disused wartime USA hospital. It consisted of a series of individual units linked together with open walkways. Many of the patients were young soldiers who had returned from the front line with horrendous injuries, shrapnel wounds, severe burns and broken bones. Some were undergoing skin grafts. Skin was often donated from the abdomen or other fleshy area and grown to the injured site by way of the forearm. The consequences of which caused the patient to be somewhat of a contortionist. Despite their terrible injuries and pain, they were full of fun, and she had a truly happy time working in this unit. These young servicemen did not worry about protocol or authority. They had nothing to lose. She smiled to herself as she recalled the evening they had chased her around the ward trying to get her on to an empty bed.

"Stop, stop! I'll be in real trouble if anyone finds me like this." She managed to escape, locking herself in the linen cupboard.

All the patients thought it was hilarious and were egging them on. She was so worried in case she was discovered behaving in such an unseemly way, but they carried on regardless for what seemed an endless time leaving her with uniform all askew. Uniforms then were worn with pride; blue and white striped dresses, stiffly starched aprons and silly caps that served no practical purpose.

One evening, when Lucy was working at the top end of the ward, she saw the consultant walk through the door at the far end, followed by two young men in white coats. They made their way round the ward and came closer to Lucy. The one nearest to her looked up, and their eyes locked momentarily. She felt a frisson of excitement and her heart missed a beat. She was instantly attracted to him. She did not know why, but adrenaline surged through her veins. Was it the way he walked or maybe it was the sparkle in his eyes? Whatever it was she had never experienced anything like this before. Her eyes followed him as the group moved slowly round the ward reading the carefully recorded details on the clipboards at the foot of each patient's bed. She observed his gentle manner and concern at what he saw. It seemed to her at that moment that he was the one for her and she would like to go out with him. He was of stocky build with tousled fair, curly hair. This must surely be love at first sight. They had never seen one another before let alone spoken to each other nor did it look as though they would without some kind of intervention. The next evening Lucy was so thrilled because the young man who had made such an impression returned.

"Heather, do you know who that good looking chap is in the white coat who's just walked in?" Lucy asked her colleague as nonchalantly as possible.

"Oh, he's a medical student. I believe there are two of them here for the summer," Heather answered with a twinkle in her eye.

"That's strange. This isn't a teaching hospital," said Lucy.

"No. I think there's some special arrangement. Probably something to do with the plastic surgery unit which as you know is a recent addition and pretty special. Anyway, why are you so keen to know?" she asked.

"I think he looks wonderful. He is so gentle and caring with the patients. I like his tousled, curly hair, too. My heart just turns over and races when I see him. Take my pulse! I bet you can't, it's beating too fast to count."

"Good heavens, I don't think he's that special. He's short and stocky and I thought you liked tall men," said Heather.

"I know but he's different. Can you fix it so that we are left alone in the kitchen after supper this evening? Please," pleaded Lucy.

Heather was a jovial character with large wide open brown eyes that twinkled as her round happy face gave way to a beaming smile. "Leave it to me."

She fancied playing Cupid.

Lucy was busy clearing away the dishes later on that evening and in walked the student. She was so surprised that she instantly dropped a plate. It went clattering to the floor, breaking into many small fragments.

"Oh dear!" was all that Lucy could muster feeling her face blush to the roots of her hair as she stood looking at the broken china pieces.

"Never mind it's only a plate. By the way I'm Patrick. What's your name?"

"I'm Lucy," she replied.

"Well, Lucy, I'll help you clear it up. D'you have to pay for breakages?"

"Not as long as it doesn't happen too often. We just have to record it in the 'breakages' book, so it doesn't look very good if your name appears too often," she answered.

They soon picked up the pieces between them.

"Thank you so much," said Lucy, but as she spoke Patrick reached across her to put the final bits in the bin and gently pushing, pinned her against the sink.

"Now I have you in a very compromising position," he chuckled.

Lucy could feel him getting harder and harder as he pushed closer to her. She hoped he could not feel her pounding heart. As she opened her mouth to say something, he instantly covered it with his and smothered her with kisses.

"Your glances didn't go unnoticed when I came through the ward yesterday. Will you come out with me tomorrow evening?" he managed to ask between the kisses.

Lucy struggled free, afraid of being caught out.

"I'd love to," she answered, trying not to sound too eager and not quite believing that this was really happening.

"You'd better leave now otherwise someone will come looking for us and that'll be bad news for both of us," Lucy continued.

She made her way back to the ward.

"It must have worked. You look as though you have really been kissed!" Heather exclaimed.

That meeting was to be the first of many secret trysts. They both had to adhere to strict duty times and Patrick was also on call if there were operations he was expected to observe. To complicate matters Lucy was moved to night duty. This restricted their meetings considerably, but they made the most of the time they managed to get together. Lucy often stayed up during the day when she should have been in bed. A 'do not disturb' notice served to keep any suspicious persons away. They devised another means of seeing one another too.

"My quarters are in the doctors' block that runs alongside your ward," Patrick said one day. "We can exchange notes through the windows if we are careful."

They exchanged billets doux and poetry that they had composed for each other and arranged dates through the windows.

During the night shift they could expect two visits from the night sister, one around ten o'clock and the other about five or six o'clock in the morning. The plastic surgery unit was the only one with wards on either side linked by a very wide enclosed passage which echoed when anyone walked down, but more importantly the clickety-clack of heels could be heard from some distance away. This served to enhance their plan.

"When night sister has done her round, I'll pull back the office curtains then you'll know it's safe to come over," Lucy suggested.

"That's a good idea."

Patrick watched for the signal which led to a number of clandestine tête-à-têtes at night. Once the patients were all in bed and after 'lights out', amid kissing and cuddling they enjoyed cups of coffee and biscuits. One night their strategy went awry. Sister paid an unexpected visit. They were only able to extricate themselves from a rather embarrassing situation by Lucy's quick thinking. She pushed Patrick into the sluice room where he endured an uncomfortable few minutes pressed behind the door as Lucy opened it to allow the night sister to reinspect.

"I'd like to look into the sluice room, Nurse."

"But you've already inspected the sluice, Sister," spluttered Lucy.

"Never mind I'll have another look."

Patrick breathed a heavy sigh of relief when she did no more than look straight in.

"Thank you, nurse, that will be all," she said giving Lucy a very quizzical look.

They suspected that she had been tipped off by another hopeful but jealous suitor, of whom there were several.

In their free time they used to go for long walks in the countryside, when time allowed, and through the woods. During this summer, the trees dressed in their bright green finery seemed to take on a special significance. The twigs crackled beneath their feet and the large roots threatened to trip them as they digressed from the pathway, looking for a soft mossy patch on which to lie wrapped in each other's arms, enjoying the precious moments. Lucy was over the moon. She was absolutely bowled over with Patrick and she was aware her feelings were reciprocated.

"I prefer to remember you as you are," Patrick said on one of many occasions when they struggled to control themselves to comply with the conventions of the times. One day he pulled out a photograph of a young lady. She had beautiful eyes and a swathe of auburn hair.

"This is the girl my parents wish me to marry. She is a Roman Catholic. It is making my relationship with you or indeed anyone else difficult. I love you and don't wish you to get hurt," Patrick explained. "You see I rely on my parents to finance my career. They have expressed their disapproval of me thinking of marrying anyone who is not a Roman Catholic."

This was a bitter pill for Lucy to swallow. She never guessed this could possibly happen. Lucy was deeply in love with Patrick, and she knew there was never going to be anyone else for whom she could feel the same way, so it was inevitable that she was going to be hurt. She knew she should have walked away as did Patrick but neither could bring themselves to do it. They both hoped things could be changed.

Before they moved North, these woods were where Lucy later walked with their Labrador. He had such sleek and shiny coat. He was difficult to control and it was a very sad day when Blossom had to be put down as the result of an injury he had sustained on one of his escapades. The vet said it was the kindest thing to do. The memories, then still very fresh, would come rushing back. Memories of that first sensual kiss, memories of the long passionate embraces and nothing had ever again come close to this, with the exception, perhaps, of Sandy who was a close second.

The summer seemed to pass so quickly.

"It's my last night tomorrow. Father's reimbursement has come through at last and I'd like to take you out to dinner. I'd like that so much."

"That's good news. Yes, I'd love to come. I'll look forward to it."

Going out to dinner then was something of an occasion. They had decided to rendezvous outside of the front entrance gate. Lucy arrived on time, all dressed up, and waited for what seemed an eternity. She was about to leave, thinking he had stood her up, when Patrick came rushing out.

"Lucy, I'm most dreadfully sorry but I've been called to stand in theatre to watch an emergency operation. I'm so disappointed and sad to let you down but there's nothing I can do about it. We could meet tomorrow afternoon before I leave for the airport."

Patrick took her in his arms and kissed her lovingly and gently before, with regret, he dragged himself away to his duty. This was such a disappointment. Their very last chance for a dinner out. It had been promised for some time, but the money did not come through. In retrospect a wise move, perhaps, by his father.

The next afternoon they met for the very last time before Patrick had to get his flight back to Ireland. This was such a romantic and memorable time. It was hot and sunny, and the sky was bright blue as they wound their way by the river to the old watermill. It was an historic place. The mill was still working and, as they approached, they could hear the rush of the millrace and the wheel turning. As the water rushed so it seemed that time, too, was rushing, bringing them ever closer to the end of their weeks together. On the ground floor with its typical old oak beams there was information about the history of the mill and of course picture postcards. Upstairs was set out with rustic tables and chairs for afternoon tea. They found a table for two in a cosy corner and Patrick ordered tea for two and a selection of cakes. Lucy chose a Chelsea bun, her all-time favourite. It looked as though it was asking to be eaten with its lovely golden, sticky, sugary surface. That was truly the nicest Chelsea bun and cup of tea that Lucy had ever enjoyed. She and her friends had eaten many at the Chelsea Tea rooms, in their mornings off-duty. They sat fondly gazing into each other's eyes and in turn keeping an eye on the clock. The hands seemed to be moving much faster than usual!

"Although this afternoon has been wonderful, and I've enjoyed it so much, it is, nevertheless, a rather sad time too because a magical summer's come to an end. In a way that makes it even more memorable," Patrick ventured as he gazed into Lucy's eyes and took her hands in his. "I'll keep in touch as I promised but remember what I told you."

"It is indeed sad. We've packed so much into our time together. It felt as though it would never end," answered Lucy struggling to keep back the tears which she was not good at. Patrick released his grip and went to pay the bill and as he did so he pulled a coin from his pocket.

"Here" he said, "keep this for good luck," giving Lucy the coin." It's an Irish silver threepence piece which is supposed to be lucky.

She tucked it away in her purse for safe keeping and treasured it for many years. After tea they walked back along the path that they had come. When they reached the end they passionately embraced and kissed goodbye. He promised to write and telephone occasionally. Patrick was true to his word. He wrote long and beautifully descriptive letters about all the things that he was doing.

Lucy recalled some of the most memorable snippets from the letters and how he opened and closed them.

Darling Lucy,

How I miss you, your dancing eyes and lovely smile.

It is the Opera Festival this week and tonight we are all going to see Madam Butterfly.

Father reserved a box.

I wish you were here. My enjoyment will be overshadowed

by your absence.

Your ever-loving Patrick.

My Darling,

Another month without you has passed.

Today I went shooting widgeon with my father, on the South Slob. The male widgeon has a lovely whistle. A flock on the wing is a wonderful sight and the male birds whistle whee-oo. We bagged a couple.

Tomorrow I am playing for the Varsity Rugby Team. I play scrum half.

Yours as ever,

Patrick

My Darling Lucy,

I am doubly sad today. Not only am I without you but my grandmother is very ill and is not expected to live more than a few days. Father and mother have gone to be with her, and I have to help in the shop. Fortunately Father has a qualified assistant who will take care of dispensing the pharmacy.

Love you as ever,

Patrick

My Darling,

My joy would be complete today if you were here. It is a very special day. I am being conferred with a First Class Degree with Honours in Medicine. So now the real work will begin.

Lucy looked for these letters in her pigeon-hole with anticipation and her excitement knew no bounds after she had received the first one. She replied with all due haste. His letters continued to arrive regularly at first, then time lapses between them increased. She kept looking for another letter, but none was forthcoming. Then one day, someone called down the corridor to her, "Telephone for you Lucy."

She almost dropped the receiver when she heard coming down the line,

"Hello, Lucy. It's Patrick here. How are you. Just a quick call to let you know that I'm coming over to play in a rugby match in a couple of weeks' time. We can meet up. I'm forewarning so you that you can organise some time off. Will write with exact details."

"Hello, Patrick. Yes, I'm fine. You bet I will organise time off. Oh, I'm thrilled to bits."

"I'll have to go now because it is an expensive call. Look forward to seeing you so much. Be there, mind."

"You bet I will."

Lucy was elated. She could hardly contain herself. Sadly, the excitement was to be short-lived for a week later she received another call to say that the match was to be in Scotland and that he would not have enough time to get down. Who knows whether this was true or not? How that situation seemed to mirror the one with Sandy, she thought. Was she perhaps a little naïve in all she was asked to believe?

She did not receive any more letters despite the fact that she herself continued to write for a while, hoping for a reply. Then at Christmas, after she had given up hope of hearing again, she received a beautiful Christmas card from him. Out of the blue, in the New Year, Lucy received this letter, still clear in her memory,

Darling,

This is the most difficult letter I have ever had to write. I feel so monstrous and such a coward because I am not able to tell you in person. This will be my last letter to you.

Life has become impossible for me. As you know my parents have never been happy about our relationship due in part to our religious differences. I cannot live any longer with divided loyalties.

I hope you will see it in your heart to forgive me and I am sure in time you will find the happiness you deserve with someone else.

Our love for one another cannot blossom without whole heartedness from us both and that I am not able to give.

Goodbye, Lucy darling.

And so Lucy had to resign herself to the fact that maybe he finally bowed to parental pressure. Lucy was left to lick her wounds. She was left with that sinking feeling in the bottom of her stomach, the feeling that everyone seems to experience when they have to accept their love is no longer reciprocated. The bottom of her world had fallen out, but life has to keep going. She carefully packed all the letters into a box which she tied up with a blue ribbon finished with large bow on the top and carefully packed the box away; a precious collection which she read and reread for many weeks to come.

Some considerable time later, she had an invitation to go to the tennis final match at Wimbledon with Jessie, a colleague, her fiancé and his pal Bob. Lucy was still feeling somewhat raw after her experience but agreed reluctantly to go along with them. She knew little about Wimbledon and had only her schooldays knowledge of the game. They left in Bob's car very early in the morning in order to arrive in time to get a parking spot. The journey took four hours. There were no motorways or dual carriageways then. They had taken a picnic hamper packed with goodies; chicken legs, sandwiches and a couple of bottles of wine. The men had saved enough money to accompany this with the traditional strawberries and cream. They were all able to enjoy a glass or two of wine. It turned out that Bob was a great tennis enthusiast as was Jessie's fiancé who had managed to procure tickets for the centre court men's final. Frank Sedgman was the defending champion. Despite her initial misgivings, Lucy thoroughly enjoyed the tennis and the company.

Bob sat next to Lucy watching avidly as the balls flew with such precision from one side of the net to the other. It was not long before she felt his arm around her back as they joined in the ooh's and ah's when the points were either lost or scored. What a day they had and that night, after a long slow drive home, Bob dropped her back at the nurse's home. Lucy had, on this occasion, obtained a late pass. Before getting out of the car, Bob asked,

"Can I kiss you goodnight?"

Lucy did not object, so he leaned over and put his arms

around her. Soon they were locked in a long and ardent kiss.

"Who taught you to kiss like that?" he asked as he loosened his hold.

Their relationship developed quickly. They went to the cinema quite often, and Bob did like to show off. One day he took Lucy sailing. She felt a little apprehensive about this, but he assured her he could sail. However, after a short while they became stuck on a mud bank and could not get moving when a small boy aged about ten years old came sailing around looking as though he had been born in a yacht and shouted, "Pull up the tailboard mister!" He took her to the best hotels for drinks and it was at The White Hart that he introduced her to Pimm's No. 1. Sometimes he would take her home but was prone to be irritable when his father sat up very late.

"Father has his sitting trousers on this evening," he would mutter under his breath.

Some nine months after this first encounter, they became engaged and six months later they married. It had been quite a whirlwind romance. Everything had been arranged and was in place for the big day. Somehow something did not seem to feel quite right to Lucy, but she was not able to put her finger on what it could be. She had not really fathomed what was underneath that showmanship. Bob was confident and experienced, but she certainly never had quite the same feeling about him that she had experienced with Patrick. Perhaps that magical ingredient was missing, but this was surely the stuff of dreams. Dreams seldom come true.

One morning Lucy decided to go up to her room. She could not get Patrick's memory out of her head, that stocky figure with the curly hair and gentle manner. She pulled out the box with the precious letters, carefully untied the big blue bow and started to read them. Unfortunately, Bob came in unexpectedly and she had no time to put them out of sight. Naturally he was curious.

"What letters are those that you are reading so avidly?" he asked as he looked over her shoulder.

Lucy had told Bob about Patrick but had never disclosed the fact that she had kept all his letters.

"While you still swoon over that romantic rubbish, I don't think we've much chance of a happy marriage. Burn the bloody things. If you don't, I'll call the whole thing off," and promptly stormed out of the room.

Lucy was in a state of turmoil and in floods of tears. She had never seen Bob angry and certainly had never heard him swear. She went downstairs and reluctantly put them on the fire one at a time. Although this destroyed the letters, the memory lived on in her heart and the treasured silver threepence piece remained in her possession.

Lucy was reflective. She wondered what kind of life she might have had if she had been able to marry Patrick. Her life no doubt would have been lived in Ireland, but she expected it would have been one where she stayed at home looking after a family and the household affairs, although probably, a little more affluent. She concluded that there was a similarity between Patrick and Sandy and the emotions that they aroused. However, she brought herself back to earth, replaced the silver coin, along with its memories, in the sweet tin and continued with the task in hand. After all her trip was not too far away now and she had to think about what clothes she would take with her. It was also a good time to discard some that she had not worn for a long time. They could go to a jumble sale. She spent the rest of the afternoon sorting clothes. Lucy busied herself for a couple of hours when she was distracted by the telephone.

Chapter 7

"Hello there, Lucy."

It was unmistakably Sandy's voice. He was not going to be easily put off, thought Lucy, as she answered. Sandy was not only feeling lonely and empty now that Helen had left again, but he had always been used to having his way with women. He thought he should be the one in command. He was not used to being kept waiting but there was something about Lucy that attracted him. Perhaps it was her vulnerability. In any event, he was pretty sure that he would eventually break down this barrier that she had built around herself. He was arrogant enough to assume that she needed him as much as he wanted her. He was sure, too, that Helen would eventually tire of this cat and mouse game they seemed to be playing with one another.

"There's a good film on tonight in town. I wondered if you would like to come with me," went on Sandy.

"You know I asked you not to get in touch with me again," replied Lucy. She knew she ought to put down the receiver, but she could not bring herself to do it. She wanted to talk to Sandy.

"Well, I wondered if you may have changed your mind," answered Sandy. "And whether you'd like to come with me to see it. Helen's still away and I am feeling a bit lonesome.

"That makes two of us then," retorted Lucy in as high-handed a manner as she could muster. "It need not have happened this way if you had played straight with me in the first place."

Lucy could feel her heart pounding in her chest. She was unsure whether this was with anger or excitement.

"I know and I'm truly sorry," replied Sandy, contritely. "I'm going to Dubai in a week for the company and don't know how long I'll be away. Thought it might be a chance to see you again before I leave."

"I did have something planned this evening and I don't know whether I can rearrange it at such short notice."

Lucy thought it would be better to keep him waiting a while. It would also give her time maybe to even harden her heart.

"See what you can do and I'll give you another call in a couple of hours."

"OK," said Lucy.

Lucy had not progressed very far with sorting her clothes. Although she did a little more, she was unable to concentrate. She kept turning the situation over in her mind. They were both rather lonely so perhaps it would not do any harm if they occasionally went out together. On the one hand she was telling him that she did not wish to see him again and now here she was not being able to say 'no' to his persistent advances. She felt that it was not the right move to make but, as so often, Lucy let her heart rule her head. She was desperately lonely and would like to have another partner. She decided in her own mind, though, that if Sandy did ring again, she would have to play a little more 'hard to get'.

Sandy did indeed ring the second time.

"OK, I'll come out with you tonight, but I'll drive myself and meet you at the cinema," Lucy agreed.

This would prevent her having to ask him in for coffee. She had no illusions as to where that would lead. The telephone rang again. This time it was Mary's husband, Malcolm.

"Hello, Lucy." He sounded distressed. "I'm ringing to let you know that Mary's in hospital. She's had emergency major surgery. She really is very poorly. She asked me to let you know."

"Oh dear, I'm so sorry. It must have been a very sudden onset."

"Well, you know what she's like. By all accounts I don't think she's been feeling on top form for some time but wouldn't go to a doctor."

"Look, I'll try to get some leave from work and come up tomorrow morning to see her and perhaps I can be of some assistance," replied Lucy.

"Are you sure? It's kind of you even to consider it," he replied.

"Oh, it's the least I can do. After all Mary's been very good to me in times of trouble." answered Lucy. Mary had always been ready to listen if Lucy chose to confide in her.

"I'll expect you sometime tomorrow then, unless I hear anything different."

"Fine, I'll be there."

Lucy stood for a moment, reflecting, before she replaced the receiver. She quickly gathered her thoughts and drove to the college.

"Hello, Lucy. It's not your class this evening is it?" said Ruth, the receptionist, pencil in hand, scrolling the student roll.

"No. I've just come to let you know that I'll be absent from classes for a while. Certainly for the next week or two. I've had some disturbing news and need to get away to help."

"Oh, sorry to hear that. We'll miss you, but just let us know when you can resume the course and perhaps we can make some adjustments to the fees."

"That's kind. Thank you, but I hope it won't be for too long."

Her painting had come on in leaps and bounds and she had discovered that she had a dormant creative streak that she was going to exploit. Next year she would enrol for a full-time interior design course, but she would need to continue with her job during the evenings for as long as possible. At present she was being called in to cover lunchtimes as well, but she was finding this too much. After all, this job had only been a temporary measure until she finally decided what career she would like to follow. Her mind was made up now. This had all happened with a chance meeting on the riverbank with Pip.

Her next port of call was the Hotel.

"Hello, Lucy. What brings you here? You're not working this evening?" asked Mrs. Hamilton who happened to be crossing the reception jangling a bunch of keys.

"No. I wonder if I could have a few words with you in private."

"Why, yes. I hope it's not bad news."

"I'm afraid it is."

"Not Richard, I hope."

"Oh no, it's a very dear friend who has, unexpectedly, had major surgery. I need to be with her for a while."

Lucy apologised for the short notice but Mrs Hamilton was understanding and told her not to worry about hurrying back.

Lucy often found herself thinking about Pip and their chance encounter. She wondered what had happened to him. No one at the college knew any more only that he was not able to return. What a shame, Lucy thought, because she had enjoyed their painting sessions so much. She supposed now she would never see him again, although circumstances often surprised her. She had grown very fond of him. He was so gentle and considerate. When she was with Pip, there was not the passion that Sandy aroused in her. Just a peaceful and pleasurable feeling without the pressure. Maybe, he was the brother that she had always wished she'd had.

She rang Sandy.

"I'm sorry, Sandy, unfortunately I've been called away. My friend, Mary's had to go into hospital for emergency surgery. Her husband's very distressed, so the least I can do is to go up and lend a hand and I'll need the evening to make some preparations."

Sandy was not impressed. Lucy knew, of course, that it was much better this way, because she was sure to allow herself to get involved again.

Lucy arrived at 'Three Chimneys' in time for lunch. Malcolm suggested they had a snack out somewhere and drive on to the hospital afterward. Mary was in a poor state, with drips and tubes seemingly everywhere. Malcolm left Lucy with Mary after a while and said he would be back for her later. Mary was too weak to talk very much but she did seem to cheer up a little before they left her again.

Driving home in the car, Malcolm turned to Lucy and said,

"The surgeon told me that Mary had been quite lucky to have pulled through the operation and her condition is stable at present. However, he warned me not to build up my hopes because there was still a long way to go. He also thought that Mary was going to need quite a long period of convalescence once she was discharged from the hospital but that was obviously not going to be for a while yet."

"Well, I suppose that's to be expected," Lucy replied.

After taking the dogs for a walk, Malcolm and Lucy went to the local pub for a meal. Everyone was very friendly and of course concerned for Mary. The publican was a jolly character, with a round face and ruddy complexion, a fount of jokes and stories. He served at the bar while his wife was in charge of the kitchen. When she came through, they engaged Lucy and Malcolm in conversation at some length and were interested to hear about Lucy's artwork.

"We could hang some of your paintings in the reception areas. We've done it for other artists in the past. It's surprising how many are sold. It gets you known."

That was quite exciting news for Lucy but she wondered whether her paintings were good enough for this. However, she supposed there was no harm in trying.

"You know, Malcolm, I don't think I can be of much help at the moment. I'll pop in to see Mary over the next couple of days, then go home. It would be more beneficial to return when she's discharged. She's going to need a lot of help at that point, and I could organise an extended visit."

"What a wonderful idea, if you're sure you can spare the time. You're right. She'll need a lot of support and I was thinking that I would have to employ help of some kind but to have someone known to us both would be special. Let's discuss it further when we've had time to think it over."

Lucy dropped into the hospital again to visit Mary before she finally left. She found Mary rather tearful.

"Come on Mary, keep your chin up. I'll come back as soon as you are ready to leave hospital. I'll be able to negotiate a longer period away from work. Look, I've brought you a bunch of your favourite flowers. There's one good thing that's come out of this. You've inadvertently kept me from making a fool of myself again with Sandy. You were right when you said 'Beware'," Lucy went on as she kissed Mary's cheek and wiped away the tears with a tissue.

It brought a very wan smile to her face.

"OK, I'll cheer up just for you," answered Mary.

***

There was a blinding flash, a scream, a screech of brakes and a resounding bang as the two vehicles collided head-on. Pip was lying in the road and Angela had been thrown onto the grass verge. The sound of the police sirens and the emergency ambulance rang in his ears. He just managed to prop himself on to one elbow when he caught sight of Angela's blood splattered body and her face, ashen white, framed by her long dark curls, before he fell back too weak and distraught to maintain his position. He was carefully lifted on to a stretcher and whisked away to the nearest hospital. Unconscious by the time they arrived at the accident and emergency department he eventually came round to a doctor leaning over him.

"You probably can't remember much about what's happened, but you've been involved in a nasty car accident."

"No, I can't remember anything other than a blinding flash and a scream," replied Pip.

"I remember that Angela, my girlfriend, was driving us home. Where is she? What's happened to her? Is she safe?" he asked as he anxiously looked around the room trying hard to focus.

"Don't concern yourself at the moment about anyone else, just think about pulling through yourself."

Pip answered in a very irascible manner.

"Of course I'm bloody worried for Angela and I've every right to know what's happened to her. Find out and tell me right away," he replied with his voice gradually rising as he struggled against his exhaustion, falling back on the pillow.

The doctor went away and returned in a short while.

"I'm afraid I've some very bad news. Brace yourself... Angela was killed outright. If it's any consolation, she died instantly and would not have known anything about the accident or felt any pain," said the young doctor, gently taking Pip's hand, knowing what an added distress this was for him to bear.

Pip had reacted badly to this. He blamed himself for her death. Whilst at a birthday party, he ignored Angela's pleas for him not to have any more alcohol and continued to drink heavily. He could barely stand when they left. Consequently, Angela had to drive. Angela had been exonerated because the oncoming driver, with whom they had collided, was prosecuted for dangerous driving. Pip always felt that had he been driving he would have been able to take avoiding action and had never forgiven himself. Angela had been his girlfriend for a long time and they planned to get married. After the accident, Pip went into a deep depression requiring psychiatric help. Painting helped him to get well, and he had continued with it. He was not able to return to his previous employment. In any case he did not wish to settle down again to office routine. He set his mind on a complete change of lifestyle. He threw himself wholeheartedly into painting. His paintings were highly thought of in the local area where he became a well-known artist.

Now, sitting in the hospital, waiting for a doctor's verdict on his mother's condition, brought the horror of that moment back to him. Even though it had been five years ago, it again became vivid in his mind. He had never thought about finding anyone else to settle with because he thought he could never love anyone as much as he had loved Angela. People told him that time would heal. He should try to move on. This always seemed to him to be a glib expression. He did not want to move on; he wanted things to remain as they were. How can anyone know or begin to understand unless they have been through a similar traumatic experience? When his father was alive, he told him that he must try to put it behind him and find a new life. His mother had told him the same thing.

"Pip, I think it's time for you to settle down. Stop roaming around in that van of yours and find yourself another girlfriend. You can't live in the past forever and neither is it healthy to keep blaming yourself. It has been proved the accident could not have been avoided even if you had been driving."

Although they did not see a great deal of one another Pip and his mother had become quite close since both Angela and his father had died. He felt responsible for his mother, particularly as her health began to fail. Pip thought now, as he anxiously awaited the doctor's verdict, that he was possibly going to lose the last person who meant anything to him. When the doctor finally emerged from behind the curtains, he told Pip that his mother needed hospital treatment but first they would need his permission. She had had another stroke and he was unsure whether or not she would survive the night. Pip thought how nice it would be to have someone to talk to, but he had shut himself away from the real world and, apart from Lucy, had no real friends. As she approached for her painting lessons, Lucy's face always broke into a beautiful smile. She was observant of detail, eager to get started and always enthusiastic. He had enjoyed teaching her to paint and was pleasantly surprised at how quickly she had picked up the art. He deduced that she must have a natural talent, albeit so far unnoticed.

It was a quiet funeral. A ray of sun managed to shine down on his mother's coffin as it reposed in front of the altar. A larger number of people than he had expected gathered in the small church to say goodbye to a highly respected figure of that small community. Pip choked back a tear and looked back on her life during which she always been there for him and others in a very quiet and unassuming way. First, he would have to remain to sort out the estate and deal with all the formalities after which he supposed he would return to his van and possibly move it on to another place. He had to give up his post at the college and his small studio. He doubted whether there would ever be another vacancy at the college and indeed whether he would be welcome again having had to leave them so unexpectedly.

***

Lucy had managed a couple of flying visits to see Mary before she heard from Malcolm that Mary was to be discharged. She selected a few of her best paintings and dropped them off at the pub on the first of these trips. Unfortunately, Mary was to have intensive periods of treatment between which she was going to require a lot of support. Lucy had been giving this a great deal of thought. She concluded that it would be good for all parties concerned, if she went up to look after Mary for as long as she needed help. This was not entirely selfless, for ever since Lucy had returned, Sandy never left her alone. While she was away from him, she was fine, but he was too much like a magnet. At the sound of his voice she melted and was just not able to resist him. She received unpleasant anonymous phone calls. It was most upsetting. Lucy assumed they must be initiated by Sandy who was increasingly frustrated by her refusals. A break away from this would be beneficial to her well-being ,too No one would know where she had gone.

Lucy made an appointment to see Mrs Hamilton the next day at two o'clock. As Lucy walked into the waiting room, Mrs Hamilton came in behind her.

“Do come through Lucy. Now to what do we owe this unexpected visit?” she asked.

“I’m so sorry, Mrs. Hamilton, but my home situation is such that I have to leave unexpectedly and I’ve come to tender my resignation. I truly am sorry about this since I enjoyed working here so much.”

“Oh, that’s a blow. We certainly loved having you and I’d put you in line for promotion.”

“That makes it even worse,” answered Lucy, “but I have to stick by my decision.”

Lucy worked out her notice at the restaurant and also said she would no longer be attending the college for painting sessions. This made her very sad, but she was sure it was the best way out of a difficult situation. She had also heard from Richard again, asking her to postpone her trip for a while, because he had been seconded to carry out a project in South America. He was not sure for how long. No less than six months but perhaps on his return they could arrange her visit. Lucy replied telling him about Mary and that for the time being she would not make any forward plans. She did not mention anything about Sandy.

Pip returned. He spent a couple of mornings down by the river, but Lucy did not show up. He also went to the college to see if by any chance there was a vacancy that he could fill but, as he expected, they were managing at present. Maybe next school year there would be something that he could apply for. He discovered, too, that Lucy had left her day classes but was not able to establish her whereabouts. How full of near misses life seemed to be! She was coming into his thoughts a lot more often. He started to feel guilty because in his mind this was being disloyal to Angela’s memory. He knew his mother would say you must not live in the past. Never forget it, but to relive it is disastrous.

Spring was approaching. Pip hitched his caravan up to his Range Rover ready to drive off the next day. He had spent the winter painting and refurbishing it ready for a trip he had long-considered. The next morning, he set off making his way northwards to Scotland. He spent some weeks touring Scotland reaching as far as Inverness. He painted lochs, rivers and mountain scenes. He thought the scenery was out of this world. The local farmers were friendly and allowed him to park on their property. Their life was hard but none the less simple, which appealed to Pip so he lingered on the mainland longer than he had first anticipated, chatting to the local people and enjoying the folklore and country tales. Before making his way Southwards again he enjoyed a show at the Festival Theatre in Pitlochry. When Pip reached Oban, he boarded the ferry for the Isle of Mull. He drove round the island drinking in the awe-inspiring scenery and could not resist the temptation to paint a picture of what is deemed the 'World's Smallest Professional Theatre'. He sketched, too, the colourful row of houses in Tobermory. A boat tour to Iona and across to Staffa beckoned. The time would be right for the puffins. The waters were turbulent, but the wonderful sight of the newly arrived birds with their red, parrot-like beaks riding the waves helped to ease the churning he felt in his gut.

Pip would like to spend the rest of his life here. There was so much to see and paint. Every time he considered it though a face with a beautiful smile loomed in front of him, pushing such thoughts from his mind. On his way home, Pip stopped in a small village in Northumberland. A country pub seemed to beckon; a place where he was warmly welcomed by the landlady and her husband who was busy throwing logs onto the large open fire with flames licking right up the chimney breast. It was a long time since he had seen a fire like this and rather enjoyed toasting his feet and fingers in the heat that shimmered above the hearth. He ordered a drink and a ploughman's lunch and sat back to enjoy the pleasant surroundings when a small collection of paintings hanging on the side wall caught his eye. What was he seeing? Could this really be what he thought it was? He took a closer look and saw what was definitely 'Lucy Barber' scrawled in the bottom right-hand corner. He could not believe his eyes. Was this the same Lucy that he had helped to get started with her painting those few days on the riverbank? Lucy who so tentatively held the paintbrush and did not know how to prevent it from dripping.

"Some interesting land- and river-scapes you have on your

walls," said Pip to the landlord who explained how he had come by them.

"Yes, we have sold a few, too, which is encouraging for Lucy."

"Does she often come in here?" asked Pip.

"Not since her friend was taken ill. I gather she is looking after her for the time being. Nice couple, but they seemed to have hit a bad patch. D'you know her then?

Vaguely," replied Pip. "Tell her Pip asked after her when she next comes in."

"Ah yes, I will."

Pip finished his ploughman's and his cider and drove off thinking to himself what a coincidence this had been. A sense of anticipation overwhelmed him accompanied by a tinge of caution.

***

Christmas came and went without either Bob or Richard, so Lucy was pleased to be able to spend it with Mary and Malcolm.

Mary had received her final treatment and continued to make excellent progress defying medical opinion.

"I'm going to do the breakfast this morning," Mary called up the stairs this morning when Lucy had overslept.

"Oh no, I'm just coming," Lucy yelled back, but when she stepped into the kitchen she could see she was too late.

"Oh, it looks as though my presence is becoming somewhat superfluous here," Lucy quipped. "It's beginning to look as though you'll soon be able to manage without me."

"Yes, that time's fast approaching."

"Give it another week, shall we say, but in any case you know where I am if you should need me again. I must say it will be good to get back to pick up some threads. It seems ages ago since I was home."

"You know we are both so grateful for your help and for putting your life on hold for me. I quite understand that you must go. You have to get on with your life. I really can't thank you enough for all the help that you have given us."

"It's been my privilege and I'm so pleased that you've made such a splendid recovery."

Lucy had of course missed Sandy but she had not given him

a contact number or address and she did not try to get in touch with him. She expected that he had found another lover. Lucy did not think that he was the sort of man to be without a woman for long. She expected that this was probably partly the reason for the rift between himself and Helen. Lucy did think that Helen was behaving in a very selfish manner though.

Lucy was weighing up her options now. She was certainly committed to enrolling for the design course at the college. She hoped to get a job in interior design once that was completed. She might also try the art galleries to see if there were any openings. This would give her some much needed experience, and also a chance to study other artists. It would certainly be preferable to taking up waitressing again unless of course her financial situation became too precarious. Another consideration was the problem of space in her house. It was very small, and she needed somewhere to work. It was inevitable that she would have to move to a larger property. This would have to be in the same town or close by because she was determined now to enrol on the course. She was certain that this was the way forward. So she resolved, on her return, that she would look into the possibility of moving.

Lucy said goodbye to Mary and Buster. She was going to miss him as much as anyone. As soon as she drove off she began to anticipate that empty feeling that she would no doubt experience, once again, when she opened her front door but on her arrival it was not as bad as she had expected. In fact, she felt for once that she would enjoy her own company. There was, after all, plenty to think about. She wondered what Pip was doing and whether he had returned to paint on the riverbank.

Chapter 8

Some years after Marjorie had deserted her family she started to recognise the distress they must have endured as a result of her actions, and becoming aware of an increasing loneliness, contacted her parents. Her mother was overwhelmed but she learned how frail her father had become.

"Oh, you're alive, thank God, but I'm not sure your pa will survive the shock. He's so weak," came her mother's voice over the airwaves.

One night, not long after this initial contact Marjorie was awakened by the telephone. She wondered who ever it could be at such an unusual hour and expected some bad news.

"Marjorie," a tearful voice faltered at the other end.

"If you want to see your father alive again you should come home now."

It was her mother, Olive. Marjorie returned to England immediately. She loved her father dearly. She reached his bedside a few moments before he took his last breath. He opened his eyes when she spoke and managed a smile. Marjorie clasped his hand as he uttered his last words to her, "Be sure to find those bairns, pet."

She was heartbroken. Her father could never reconcile the breakup of his daughter's first marriage. He could not bear to think that she had abandoned her children and always thought of his grandchildren as the children he remembered when Marjorie disappeared. They had not had any contact since their mother left and began to believe that Marjorie had lost her life in some way.

Marjorie initially remained with her mother and together they took steps to see whether they could trace the children and perhaps, although she dared not set her sights too high, even see them again.

Marjorie and her mother decided to return to the town where she had lived, prior to that fateful day when she had packed her bags and left. Marjorie had always intended to go back but then could never find the courage. They thought that this might serve as a good starting point to do some research into establishing the whereabouts of her children. It was never going to be easy though. They arrived by train one very wet and cold winter's evening. "Let's take a taxi to the hotel, Mother," Marjorie said, shivering and wrapping her scarf higher around her neck. She was still feeling the cold even after living in a colder country for so long. She hailed a taxi and they both climbed in, pleased for the shelter and warmth that it offered against the murky weather outside.

"Oh, that's better," sighed her mother, relieved to feel the heat in the cab.

Marjorie was concerned for her mother because despite her robust appearance she suffered with her chest and by this time was coughing a great deal and looked very pale. They arrived at their hotel where they were ushered to a comfortable room. Soon they were tucking into a hot meal and the colour soon began to return to Olive's cheeks. Marjorie heaved a silent sigh of relief.

A few cursory inquiries around the area where Marjorie had lived brought disappointment. She called in at the hair salon where she had been a regular client and a friend of the owner's sister. The bell gave its usual tinkle as she opened the door, but inside things were very different. The washbasins had now been changed to backwash and the smell of permanent waving no longer wafted through the air. There were a couple of young people having highlights and one elderly lady with a blue rinse. One of the hairdressers called, "Have a seat. Be with you in a moment." Marjorie sat on the plush sofa that had replaced some of the old chairs and waited while the latest client paid her bill.

"Would you like another appointment, Betty?"

"I'll make one later, thank you," Betty replied, looking quizzically at Marjorie as she spoke. "Your face looks familiar, love. I'm sure I've seen you before but can't place you." Before Marjorie had time to answer she had made her way out of the salon.

Marjorie could not recall the face, so her hopes of getting a lead there were dashed almost before they had taken hold. The senior stylist came over and sat next to Marjorie, "The salon changed hands several years ago and I can't tell you where the previous owner's gone. She did say something to me before she left about a friend of the family going away and leaving her children but I've no knowledge of their whereabouts. I'm so sorry I can't help you and I don't know anyone who can."

"Thank you very much for your help. I think we'll probably return home and try to find other sources for help. Thank you again," Marjorie replied, shaking hands with the stylist.

A further disappointment, but then Marjorie thought about the newsagents.

"We heard that Tom remarried and went to live on the Isle of Man. The children initially went with him, but they did come back for holidays from time to time with their grandparents. They've both passed on now, but at their funeral, your children, teenagers by then, were heard saying that they were going to seek out their mother. Whether or not they did, I couldn't say."

After a disappointing two weeks, Marjorie and her mother decided to leave for home the next day, but before leaving, Marjorie took a walk down the street where she had lived to take a last look at the old house. It was almost unrecognizable, with an extension to the rear and an imposing conservatory in the front. The lawn, beautifully manicured, was surrounded with well-kempt flower borders. It was in stark contrast to the garden they used to have. Neither she, nor Tom, liked gardening, so the garden had been used as a play area for the children. With a heavy heart, she turned and started to walk back up the road when she saw through a veil of tears, a familiar looking figure coming towards her. Was it... could it possibly be Bob?

"Good heavens! Look who's here. A wonderful surprise. How lovely to see you, Marjorie, but what brings you here after such a long time?" he asked in his usual laid-back manner sucking away at his pipe.

"Oh my goodness, fancy meeting you of all people," blurted Marjorie, completely taken aback. "I'm looking for my children; those two beautiful twin boys I so callously deserted . How I long to see them to give them a hug. I've never stopped thinking about them, wondering what they look like, where they are and what they're doing. I'm so ashamed and guilty I've never had peace of mind." From her bag, she pulled a black and white photograph, "This is all I have to remember them with, they were so small. I wonder if they still have curly hair. It was so pretty and they had such impish grins and lots of freckles."

Taking another draw on his pipe, Bob replied, "Life must have been tough for you to leave them like that. They'll be in their twenties now."

Marjorie remembered that Lucy always claimed that she knew where Bob was because of the well-known smell of tobacco. He had put on a great deal of weight and had lost much of his hair and what was left was greying. He did not come across as being a happy man.

"Rumour had it that you had a transfer to York."

"Yes, that's correct, but Lucy and I had a divorce. After an unsuccessful attempt to live with the girl who was responsible, in part, and another more unsatisfactory liaison, I decided to make a clean break and return to the old roots. What have you been up to then all this time? You certainly left everyone guessing and didn't mean to be found," answered Bob.

"Tom and I had a terrible row. He always suspected that you and I were having an affair and I couldn't convince him otherwise. The row on that fateful evening stemmed largely from his unfounded jealousy."

***

"I've had nothing to do with him and I shouldn't have to ask you every time I need a new dress whether I can buy one. I'm off," cried Marjorie as she rushed up stairs slamming the door behind her.

Tom took the stairs two at a time as he made after her. Just as she reached the bedroom, he caught her sleeve and pulled her back. He had a really wild look in his eye and from experience she knew what was going to happen.

"Stop, stop. Please stop, please stop."

She lifted her other arm and gave him one hard slap across his face.

He was so surprised that he released her sleeve, spontaneously putting his hand to his face wondering how she had mustered so much strength. Marjorie had never retaliated like this before. It was so unexpected. They had had many rows, usually about finances and purchasing new clothes for the many events with which Tom's work brought them into contact. More recently, though, he had detected a change in her and suspected that she was having an affair. This was not so, although Marjorie was happy to give that impression. Indeed, she had been attracted to Bob but that is where it had remained even though she thought that he had more than friendly feelings for her.

"You go then, if that's what you want, but you'll not get custody of the twins."

"I'd like to, but despite our loveless marriage I'm pregnant again, so all such thoughts are meaningless."

Marjorie knew this would be his reaction and she knew too that he would fight hard to keep them. She had no job and no prospects, having left school without any qualifications so it would be impossible to mount a challenge. It was the worst day of her life when, at breaking point she made the final decision to leave. She knew that she could not give the children the home or financial support that their father could afford so she made the heart-breaking decision not to take them. She knew, too, that she would also be up against her in-laws.

Marjorie's father had worked at the coal face. As a family they had faced many difficult times. Money was always short and there was little for food, and certainly nothing spare for good clothes. Their clothes were usually purchased from jumble sales. Often the better ones were pawned at the beginning of the week and redeemed on Saturday morning after pay day. They wore them for the weekend then pawned them again on Monday. Marjorie remembered her father coming home, black with coal dust, having to wash down in an outside tub. Sometimes, at the end of a shift, the men would take a bath together in the communal one at the pit head. Their two up two down did not have a bathroom and the outside toilet was shared. Their food was basic and at the end of the week there was often little left to eat. Tom came from a wealthier background and this probably accounted for the fact that Marjorie fell head over heels for him. It was the lifestyle that she liked. She grew increasingly extravagant and Tom did not always agree about what she should buy. He was also very possessive, and Marjorie needed to be more independent, something she had never been and something that eventually came at a great cost.

Their love-making took place only after Tom had been out drinking, when she could not shake him off. "I'm going up to bed. I have a headache and I'm not feeling too well."

"Here we go. Same old story. I know you don't want me to make love to you."

"It's not that at all. You just don't understand."

"Huh, doesn't take much understanding. It's always the same pattern. I know there's another man."

Marjorie could not bear him to approach her and just put up with his advances as a duty. If he tried to put his arms around her, she struggled free and turned her back to him. He was so gauche. It was true that she had met someone else, but that was a long time ago. Tom had hit her on more than one occasion, but he never touched the children.

"You sneaky little bitch," he yelled as he hit her. "I saw you walking with a man who looked like Bob earlier this evening as I drove back from the office. You told me you were going to meet Audrey for a coffee and who should you be with but that fellow from up the road."

Marjorie ignored the jibes and went upstairs to bed but, as she came from the bathroom, Tom shouted,

"Suppose it's his child you're carrying."

"That's madness and you've no grounds for thinking it." Marjorie retorted and with that he gave her a shove. She lost her balance and fell to the bottom of the stairs. She was stunned for a moment. She tried to move but her head just spun. Tom made to go to her assistance, but she managed to find the energy and the courage to tell him to leave her. Then she felt a warmth and a sudden gush from between her legs, "Oh my God. Call a doctor. I've lost the baby."

Marjorie lay at the foot of the stairs bleeding profusely clutching her skirt around her to try to soak the blood and water. She tried to sit up, but when she moved she bled more profusely.

"Now it doesn't matter who was the father because I've lost the baby anyway," she sobbed. "Thanks to your stupidity."

"It was your fault. You tripped on purpose I suppose."

Marjorie knew he would blame her and by this time she was in a lot of pain and too weak to argue further while they awaited medical help. As she passed out, she thought 'thank goodness I am going to die.'

After her recovery she was told by a specialist that it was a million to one chance that she could conceive again. This did nothing to help cement their relationship. Like many women in this situation, she threatened to go but always returned. Things would eventually calm down and a new dress or an outfit and a dinner out did much to help on a superficial level. This time it did not work. Friends and neighbours were shocked when they heard she had left because on the surface they looked to be a well-suited couple.

***

"I know quite a nice little pub where we can get a drink. We can have a good chat and catch up with all that has happened," said Bob.

"That sounds like a good idea. What about Mum? I left her at the hotel."

"Bring her with you. I'll walk back with you."

Marjorie told Bob that after spending a few weeks with a friend she did contact her previous lover and eventually flew out to Canada with him. He had served in the Royal Canadian army during the war. As a result of serious injury in Normandy he had been evacuated by ship to England where he received treatment and remained. He was considerably older than Marjorie but was quite affluent. After a stressful and challenging time obtaining her divorce, Marjorie and her Canadian lover married but the marriage soon faltered. Bob thought that given the circumstances, coupled with the trauma and guilt that Marjorie had experienced as a result of abandoning her children, no doubt brought about its demise. She said that she had continued to live in Canada being well supported by her ex-husband. Tom meanwhile, had obtained a divorce on grounds of his wife's desertion and had remarried.

"Do you remember Bob, Mum? An old friend from long ago. We just bumped into one another. Thought we might go for a drink and a chat. Would you like to come with us?"

"That'd be lovely," replied Olive.

"The weather's not particularly good for walking, so how about I go for the car and we can drive there."

"That will be much better. Especially for Mum who has a problem with her chest."

"Who is your friend?" asked Olive. "I don't really remember him."

"They used to live at the top of our road years ago. Their son, Richard, was a friend of our boys."

Bob returned with his car. They bundled in and drove off.

"What would you like to drink?" asked Bob.

"I think it would be more appropriate to have a hot cup of coffee. It will warm us up."

Bob had a beer. They had a good chat over their drinks. Marjorie followed her coffee with a cherry brandy.

"Perhaps you can throw some light on the whereabouts of the children," Marjorie said to Bob in a hopeful tone. "We've been here for two weeks and haven't managed to get anywhere with our search."

"Afraid not, but I will do all I can to help."

At breakfast the next morning, Marjorie's mother stared into her cup of tea. "You know it felt so strange bumping into Bob like that. He didn't have too much to say about himself. Wonder what he's been up to all these years. His face certainly lit up on seeing you. D'ye know Marjorie, I'd like to go home. I really don't feel well enough to be of much use here. You stay and perhaps you and Bob will have some luck in tracing the whereabouts of those bairns."

"Well, are you sure that's what you want, Mum? I'll miss your company, y'know."

"Yes, that's what I'd like to do. Contact our Jim and get him to meet me off the train."

They took Mum to the station the following day, after contacting Marjorie's brother to meet her. So it was that Marjorie's mother returned home and Marjorie stayed with Bob. He promised to help find the children. They drove to his house which he had furnished very comfortably and the two of them chatted well into the early hours of the morning over a couple of bottles of wine, catching up on all that had happened during the intervening years.

"As I mentioned briefly, Lucy and I had a divorce some years ago now. I had a couple of relationships but, sad to say, neither of them lasted. So here I am on my own," Bob explained to Marjorie. "I think that the memories of Lucy were too vivid at the time, despite our apparent incompatibility. I acted too rashly and wish that we were still together, but I don't suppose Lucy will feel that way, otherwise she would have contacted me. Richard tells me that she is still on her own, though, despite a couple of suitors."

Many of Marjorie's friends had inevitably moved away but she discovered there were one or two remaining. She set out the following day to look up some of them, but none could throw any light on what had happened to her children. Marjorie and Bob tried every avenue but to no avail. They had so little information on which they could rely. Finally, finding the pain of disappointment too much to bear, Marjorie became so disheartened that she decided to give up the search. She was also of the opinion that it was not right to rely any longer on Bob's goodwill. She told him that she must return to her mother where she would try to find some employment. Marjorie knew her mother would appreciate her company and a little help.

Bob was not surprised to find himself downcast about this. He had always had strong feelings for Marjorie but that was, after all, a long time ago. Even now he still found her dark, sad eyes, her pretty face and chic contours irresistible. Not entirely to her surprise, he took her into his arms and gave her a gentle loving kiss.

"You've no need to leave," he told Marjorie.

The proposition was very tempting to Marjorie, but she was not about to be immediately taken in by this. From experience this kind of attraction led to disaster, although she did think this was a genuine feeling, despite the fact that he still had feelings for Lucy. However, she adhered to her plan and returned to her mother. She and Bob decided to keep in contact and possibly meet up on the odd occasion. Meanwhile, he promised to do all that he could to continue with the search for her family.

Marjorie had to look for employment but could only manage to get part time jobs in the hospitality business which neither gave enough income nor satisfaction. She looked forward to Bob's telephone calls and did indeed find herself missing him. The next time Bob rang Marjorie ventured,

"I've spent hours in the employment exchange. It's simply soul destroying and there is nothing available that I'm suited to. I'm at my wit's end."

Bob had a pal who managed a group of furniture stores and he knew there was a representative's job becoming vacant and suggested that he put her name forward. She agreed to this.

Marjorie now found herself in a large new showroom. She had always had a flair for furnishing rooms and here she was in her element. She stayed with Bob while she looked for somewhere of her own. This was certainly something she had not expected to do, and she did wonder whether the memories of the old home would be too painful for her to cope with, but she thought that by some chance she might be able to pick up a trail on her children. Her mind was really set on this to be loyal to her father's memory and to the promise she had made him.

***

Lucy returned to her flat. She was not disappointed to find that her feelings were as she expected. The emptiness was even more stark after being with company for so long but on the other hand, she would have space and time to collect her thoughts and decide on her plan of action. There was no communication from Sandy. She secretly hoped that there would be but the fact that there was no letter or recorded telephone message made her resolve not to contact him even stronger. It would be asking for trouble to open up the relationship again after what had been a considerable break. The strong emotional feeling remained but she was convinced that it could not lead anywhere until he had severed his marriage ties, which she thought he was not strong enough to do. So, better, at this stage, to leave well alone. Her thoughts kept harking back to Pip, but he seemed to have disappeared from the area completely.

Lucy went into the kitchen and made herself a cup of coffee, curled up on the sofa and tucked into one of her favourite cream cakes that she had purchased on her way home. Fattening, she thought to herself, but good comfort food, although she was conscious that she should not indulge herself too much. She did after all want to keep her figure!

Lucy deliberated for some time and finally decided that her prime objective was to get enrolled at the College of Art for the interior design course in which she wished to become qualified. On her way the next morning she did wonder whether Pip had returned, or whether anyone had some news about him, but thought it unlikely. The term commenced at the beginning of October, so she had time to seek out larger premises. Lucy called in at several estate agents on her way to find out what was currently on the market. She also needed to know the current market prices because she would have to sell her own flat to help finance another purchase. Some looked quite promising. However, after giving it a great deal of thought, she decided not to proceed at this time. She thought that if she successfully completed the course and found employment elsewhere, she would have to move again, so she abandoned the idea for the present. She was of course now able to use the facilities at the college. It would no longer be necessary to take large pieces of work home, which had been one of the reasons behind the move originally.

The three years at college soon slipped by for Lucy. She was really settled. She applied herself diligently and was also able to obtain part time work in a local art studio. Here she obtained valuable experience and her creative ability in displaying paintings and various other artefacts was very welcome. This not only gave her vital experience but also helped finance the project. However, she did have to postpone her trip to see Richard. She felt at the time that it was probably a little early to be thinking of a big trip like that but, in any event, it had been more important to her to get through this course. Perhaps now she could start thinking about her holiday again.

Meanwhile, Marjorie and Bob explored every avenue they could think of but did not get any further with their search. Marjorie became more and more depressed about the situation. Time seemed to be slipping by. One year turned into two and two into three. Marjorie could see that she was just drifting. She visited her mother regularly and the day Bob met her on her return from such a visit, he sensed that she was very depressed.

"I have prepared a good curry for this evening's meal. Will you come and help me eat it?" Bob asked.

"Thank you. I'd love to. It'll certainly be better than sitting on my own wallowing in self-pity," replied Marjorie.

Marjorie said little during the whole evening and Bob became quite worried about her.

"What's wrong, Marjorie? Is there anything I can do to help?" asked Bob.

"No. Not really. It's just that I have made such a mess of my life. I've two failed marriages, lost my children, cannot keep a promise to my father and the memories around here are becoming unbearable. I am desperately unhappy. I wish I'd listened to my parents. They begged me not to marry Tom. Father said he just didn't trust him. I'll have to move away, but it seems thankless after you have been so kind to me. I don't know where I can go and even if I do whether I'll obtain any peace of mind," Marjorie poured out.

She knew deep down she loved Bob but tried to conceal her feelings. This had been a contributing factor to her unhappy marriage all those years ago. She thought that he guessed but nothing was ever said.

Bob wrapped his arms around her and felt an overwhelming surge of sadness creep over him. He could not bear to see her like this. She just sobbed uncontrollably.

"I don't have to say how much I love you. You know," he replied, "I'll do anything I can to make things easier for you."

"That makes it worse. I appear to be so ungrateful."

Marjorie buried herself even closer into Bob's arms. She loved him but had tried so hard to keep a distance because she was afraid that there would be a repeat of the previous situations. Neither had a good track record. Everything now had built up and things were beginning to get out of control. She could feel herself growing weaker and giving way to the strength of his embrace. He gently pushed back her hair and he kissed her forehead tenderly and then each cheek. He pressed his lips against hers and he could feel her resistance give way as he kissed her.

"Let's go up to the bedroom," Bob murmured, picking up the slight figure in his arms and carrying her upstairs.

She undressed and slid beneath the sheets. Bob followed. Their bodies wrapped together oozing warmth and strong emotion. He kissed his way down the soft skin of her abdomen until he felt the bushy growth under his lips. She had waited so long for this and finally her resistance had snapped.

The next evening, after work, Marjorie walked round to Bob's house. They sat down on the sofa together discussing their future. Bob proposed to Marjorie. She did not need any time to think and readily accepted his offer. He thought that it would be a good idea if he tried to get a transfer to the West country where they could start afresh and hopefully where eventually some of the painful memories of the past would be erased.

***

Lucy successfully completed her course and was taken on full time at the studio. This gave her immense pleasure. Now she had a regular salary with commission on anything that she sold. She was also able to continue with her own painting, but her ambition was to set up her own interior design business. Before she could do this, she would have to save some money. She advertised her expertise in the local paper, and also obtained contacts through her work so that she could start from home in her spare time.

One evening on her way home, Lucy bumped into a colleague from The White Horse where she used to work.

"D'you ever see anything of Sandy," she asked in the course of their conversation.

"I understand that he is abroad working on a three-year contract which must soon be coming to an end, or up for renewal, but don't start setting your sights on him again. Better let him be. He doesn't seem to be much good to anyone."

"Oh, come on, that's a bit harsh," retorted Lucy a little upset by this outburst, which she thought was totally out of place.

Still there was no sign of Pip. It seemed that they had both drifted out of her life, but deep down her feelings were unchanged.

Lucy had a week's holiday to come so she decided to go to Northumberland and see Mary. She had not seen a great deal of her since her recovery because she had been too busy with her course and part time work which she had to keep going to help with its financing.

Mary and Buster both welcomed her and it was good to breathe the clean salt air of the Northumberland coast.

"Lucy," Mary called up the stairs, as Lucy was unpacking her bags, "Let's take Buster for a walk and then call at the pub for lunch."

"Sounds like a good idea to me," Lucy called down, "I won't be long."

"Take your time. There's no hurry."

They went for a drink at the pub where Lucy's paintings had been exhibited. There were only a couple of them left so that gave Lucy a nice little nest egg. She wished that she had thought of bringing some more but perhaps another time. Things really seemed to be looking up now.

"We had someone called Pip in here, oh, some time ago now. He asked after you. He was making his way back home after a protracted period away. He called in on the way up. I think you just missed him."

Lucy's heart gave a little jump.

"Oh, yes, he's the one who introduced me to painting." She did not enlarge upon the subject but secretly wondered whether there was a possibility of meeting him again.

Chapter 9

Sophie looked at her watch, time was creeping on. She had not expected to get held up in so much traffic, but she calculated that she would reach the airport in time if there were no more hold-ups. She had already checked that the flight would be on time. Finally, Sophie reached the airport and parked the car. She rushed across to the arrivals her heart beating fast. It was six months since she had waved Richard goodbye, and it had seemed like an eternity. She had missed him so much. Although he had written to her, and phoned her regularly, she wondered whether his feelings towards her would have changed. Then she spotted a tall, bronzed, handsome figure coming towards her. She ran forwards, falling into his outstretched arms, and at that moment she knew that if anything their feelings for one another were even stronger.

"Oh Richard, how I've missed you!" she struggled to speak the words as Richard's bear-hug siphoned the air from her lungs.

"Darling Sophie! You look wonderful, more beautiful than ever. It is so good to be back with you. Six months is a long time when you love someone as much as I love you."

"How was South America?" she asked, not being able to take her eyes away from him.

"Grand! And guess what. I've secured a promotion and have been offered a really good position as a result when my other contract comes up for renewal."

"That's wonderful news."

"Enough about me. Let's get out of this place and then we can focus on you and what you have been up to in my absence. I hate all these crowds of people jostling for space and it's so hot. Is the car far?"

"No, I managed to park it just outside in the short stay park. We had better not linger too long otherwise we'll overstay our time," replied Sophie.

"Let me help you with some of your luggage. You seem to have returned with a lot more than you had when you left," she laughed wrestling a bag from him.

"Isn't that usually the way? All those gifts for various people you know," he answered with a twinkle in his eye. With that they drove to Richard's flat chattering about all the events that had happened, both so excited.

"Unfortunately I have to be on call tonight and have to take the early shift tomorrow. I wasn't able to get the time off because of staff shortages," said Sophie. "But I have organised a special dinner for us tomorrow evening to celebrate your homecoming—and of course now your promotion—at that first-class restaurant that's been highly recommended to me by a friend."

"How wonderful! Of course, that's typical of you. So thoughtful," answered Richard taking Sophie into his arms once more, "and this time I'm not going to let go so easily," he continued as he whisked her through to the bedroom.

Richard thought that during their dinner the next day would be the ideal time to propose to Sophie. A lovely surprise and something that they had discussed on a number of occasions but with Richard's unexpected departure they had not yet made a formal engagement. He went out that day and bought a ring. He already had a good idea of the kind of ring she would like. They both arranged to take a cab to the restaurant where they would meet. In this way they could both have a drink.

"Sophic, you look wonderful," Richard greeted her as she went up the steps to meet him.

He put his arm around her waist as they were ushered to their table. Richard had called in advance and ordered champagne. This was to be a really special evening.

The waiter brought along a bottle of champagne and after the usual ritual he poured two glasses and placed the remainder back into the ice bucket. Whilst waiting for the menu they drank a toast to Richard's success. After taking a few sips, Richard placed his glass back on the table. He looked straight into Sophie's glowing face and, reaching across the table, he took her hands in his and, ever the romantic, in heartfelt tones asked, "Darling Sophie, I do love you so much. Will you marry me?"

This was out of the blue and quite unexpected. At first, she was lost for words and poor Richard thought momentarily that he had spoiled his chances, but when the words had actually sunk in Sophie whispered with great pleasure,

"Of course I will. I love you too." The expression on her face said everything. She was just not able to stop the tears, tears of pure joy. Richard gently placed her hands on the table.

"Now close your eyes."

From his back pocket he pulled a small black velvet box placing it into her palms. She opened it to reveal a beautiful ring with diamonds and emeralds in a gold setting. Sophie's eyes opened wide and the tears of joy gave way to such a big smile.

"Richard! It is absolutely beautiful. What a wonderful surprise."

She was indeed happy. That was good reason, then, for another toast to their future happiness. They chose to walk home both feeling inwardly glowing from good food, wine and enjoying the romance of the warm moonlit evening. It seemed perfect. Nothing else mattered to them at this moment. They decided to wait a while before holding the wedding ceremony because there were many factors to take into account, not least where they would settle and the spread of their families.

***

Dusty the retriever dog was barking furiously. This usually signalled the arrival of the postman.

"Be quiet, Dusty," called Patrick, annoyed at having been disturbed from pondering over an article in the Lancet.

"'Bout time you learnt to control that dog of yours, Patrick. He barks loud enough to waken the dead," he called out as he passed the open window where Patrick was working.

"What have you brought for me this morning then?" answered Patrick. "The usual bills and junk mail?"

"No. Judging by the stamp and the post mark it looks a great deal more interesting," replied the postman as he handed him a letter sent from Australia.

Patrick recognised Sophie's handwriting. Sophie was his only daughter. Since the death of his wife Elizabeth, Sophie's mother, he had relied on her more than he realised. Patrick carefully placed the letter on the table while he went for a cup of coffee before sitting back in his study ready to enjoy reading her news. Sophie always wrote interesting and humorous letters that were a joy to read. He missed Sophie with her limitless energy and infectious laugh. He had always had a very close bond with her and, with her mop of auburn hair and striking good looks, she reminded him so much of his dear wife. His mind wandered back to that fateful day....Elizabeth was riding home after her usual morning ride on her beloved horse Pegasus when it appeared, according to a passer-by, that an impatient car driver had sounded his horn several times as he approached. Pegasus had behaved unpredictably, rearing up and throwing Elizabeth into the road. She never recovered consciousness. Sophie had left soon after the tragic death of her mother. Her trip had been planned well in advance of the accident and they had both been looking forward to travelling out to visit for a couple of months, but all that was changed now.

He was proud that Sophie had chosen to follow in his footsteps to pursue a career in medicine. He had specialised in cancer care after the death of his mother and was now a busy consultant travelling to London on a regular basis. He had a clinic in Harley Street for his private patients. He also had an apartment in the city but was always much happier when back in his native home enjoying the wonderful countryside and all the surprises that nature could bring. Patrick thought back to his training days and realised how much greater the opportunities were today for young people. He was thinking how certain events generally shaped the course of life and how particular events had steered him. Now, back in his childhood home that had been left to him by his father, deep in the Irish countryside where he was able to relax from all the traumas that his work threw at him, he remembered all too clearly the happy days that they had spent together before his mother died. The farm was a large one, but they had had a manager which left them plenty of time to go off shooting and fishing. He loved the grouse shoot but particularly enjoyed the pigeon and widgeon shooting. He also loved all the animals on the farm, taking a great interest in them. His first ambition as a child was to become a vet but then the traumatic death of his mother from cancer changed all these ideas. He vowed that he would take up medicine and try to do research into the cause of this dreadful disease.

"Mama, I don't think it's fair that you have to be so ill and suffer like this. You have always been so good, and you tell us how good God is, so why does he let this happen. I don't understand. I promise you I shall be a doctor when I grow up instead of a vet. Then I can perhaps stop this from happening to other people. I don't think it is right that people have to suffer like you have done."

He kept the promise he had made to his mother. Her drawn pale face and emaciated body still haunted him after all these years. She did not complain, despite the pain. Patrick felt this was because she held a deeply religious conviction from which she obtained a great deal of comfort.

"Patrick, come and sit with me for a little while. I can't get up today."

"Yes Mama, I will. Would you like me to read to you?"

Patrick remembered the times that he sat with his mother reading to her after she had become bedridden and, latterly, how he just sat to keep her company when she became too tired to listen or to speak. She was thankful for the companionship and the peace that this afforded. He was the only person with her when she eventually died. His father reached home just too late. He had been out with the vet to attend to the birth of a foal. It all left an indelible impression on one so young. Ironically, it was his younger brother who went on to be the vet and who now had a thriving practice.

Patrick graduated from Trinity College Medical School, Dublin and studied further at Harvard in the States before travelling to England to gain yet more experience in his field. He thought back to the time he spent prior to his graduation in a small hospital in the South West. He remembered with fondness the many nurses that he had met and, since this was just after the war, many of them were German and some were Irish. There was however always one little English girl in particular, with long, blond hair and cornflower blue eyes, who came to the forefront. He had met her accidentally but on what he was sure later had been a set up. Nevertheless, they did go out together and had also had some escapades which almost landed them in trouble. He wrote to her for some time after he left but he knew there could be no future in their relationship. His parents had already been instrumental in placing a very pretty Irish colleen in his way. She later became Sophie's mother. He wondered sometimes how different his life could have been if he had followed his instincts, but there would always have been the issue of his Roman Catholic faith.

Patrick sat back with a steaming cup of coffee on his desk and with a pearl handled letter opener sliced open the letter. It made surprising and interesting reading. Sophie had met a really nice guy whom she had been going out with regularly unbeknown to her father, although this was bound to happen, he thought. She was an extremely attractive and clever girl, just like her mother. His name was Richard and they had just become engaged. They did not plan to marry yet but hoped that it would not be too far in the future. Richard was committed to a company in Australia but had been recently offered another posting in South America once his contract in Australia had finished. She also wished to continue for another year at least. It was all very exciting. They were not certain yet where they would like to settle down, or when, but of course the wedding would be in her home-town in Ireland. Although Patrick knew that his daughter would not have any difficulty in finding a suitable partner, this was like a bolt out of the blue. He read the letter again to fully assimilate its contents. He heard the back door open. Martha, his more than competent housekeeper, called,

"Hello, Patrick. Are you there?"

"I'm in my study reading a letter from Sophie," he answered. "And guess what. She and Richard, that boyfriend she mentioned before, have just become engaged."

"Well, that's exciting news. Have they arranged a date for their wedding?"

"They are waiting at least a year apparently. How sad it is that her mother's not here to share the news, and even more so to oversee the wedding preparations."

"It is a sad thing, but we must focus on the happier aspects. Don't you be worrying yourself about preparations. I'll do all that for you," said Martha in her most commanding voice.

"I'm confident Martha, that all will be well in your capable hands and I've no doubt that Miss Sophie will welcome your expertise, too."

Nevertheless, Patrick wished with all his heart that Elizabeth was still with them to share the occasion. He knew also that Sophie would feel the same.

***

Bob finally secured a transfer to Devon. He and Marjorie both took a holiday. They drove down to Devon to have a look around the area hoping to find somewhere to live. They spent a happy two weeks exploring the coastline with its wonderful little coves and bays. Bob found that Marjorie's depression was beginning to lift but no matter what he was able to offer her or do for her, the loss of her children was something that she would have to come to terms with.

The time came for the move to Devon. There was excitement coupled with a little sadness, since for Marjorie it was the final cutting of the ties that had made her return in the first instance. Perhaps this really would bring closure, but she knew that she would always hope to see her two children again. She also had to ask herself whether they would wish to see her. She would at least be able to put her side of the story to them.

Things seemed to be going well for both of them. Marjorie was at peace with herself at last. They had made new friends and had many acquaintances too. This meant that they had developed quite a good social life. Then Marjorie began to feel tired for no apparent reason. This went on for a couple of months until Bob finally persuaded her to see her GP. When she returned she said, "I think that you had better sit down."

Bob immediately thought the worst but was very surprised to hear what Marjorie was about to say.

"Well, I'm expecting our baby." Marjorie did not know how Bob would take this news. This was something that they had not factored into the equation.

"That's wonderful but I'm a bit bewildered because you were told that you couldn't have any more children."

"Apparently it's one in I don't know how many chances that it has happened. It's a shock to me rather than a surprise. Of course I'll have to take great care if I'm to carry the baby to full term."

"It's going to be an experience for me too," said Bob. "I'll be, quote, an 'old dad'! More like a grandfather than a father," he said jokingly.

"I wonder what Richard will think?"

"There's that too," replied Marjorie, "but I don't suppose it'll worry him too much."

"No, especially as he has to make plans for his own wedding and future home."

Marjorie took good care to do all the things that she was told to do and of course had regular check-ups and did everything she could do to try to prevent another miscarriage. She was quite old to be having another baby being only a few years younger than Lucy. They both agreed that they would not tell anyone at this juncture until they were certain that everything was going to be alright.

***

Pip had made his way slowly back from Scotland. He had much to ponder. Going to Scotland was a digression for him. He made several visits. He hoped that he would be able to lay the ghosts of the past to rest. He thought, what a coincidence it was that Lucy had frequented the very pub where he had stopped. He deliberately chose not to linger at that time because his emotions were very mixed up and he was unsure what he really wanted, but on the way back he consciously decided to call in to find out whether Lucy was still in the area, or at the very least had called back again. He discovered, of course, that she had returned more than once and that her paintings were still being sold. This pleased him because perhaps it meant that she was still around.

Pip had received a moderate legacy from his mother, and he wondered whether he might put it towards buying himself a small house. He considered what his mother had told him and thought perhaps that she was right. He needed to live in something more solid than a caravan and put down some roots. He had to stop blaming himself for Angela's death and move on. He also had to consider the fact that he was getting older. He suffered with mild arthritis and felt that his present lifestyle was not helping the condition. Since he was a free agent he had to decide where to settle.

This question made him begin to think more seriously about Lucy. He was certainly very fond of her, although that was all he could say at the moment. He did think however, that this fondness had been reciprocated but whether it was a sufficient base for something more lasting to develop he was unsure. He thought, too, that unless he met her again, he would never be able to find out. Pip often went for a drink in the local pub which was wherever he happened to be at the moment. He had worked in the college too and had met a number of young women, most of whom were eligible, but he did not develop any feelings other than a passing acquaintance with anyone. The memory of Angela was always in the back of his mind and no one ever measured up to her. Lucy had been the only person that he had had serious thoughts about. He found these thoughts drifted into his head when he was least expecting them. He was also reminded of the other fellow, Sandy, he thought Lucy called him, who seemed to preoccupy her at the time.

Lucy was busy now. She was working at the studio during the day and was beginning to get clients for her interior design business that she was starting. She had placed her flat on the market, hoping to get a good price for it, because she had seen a house which was just what she wanted. She thought with her full-time salary and extra money that she earned from her interior design she could finance a small mortgage. She had trudged around for a long time before she found what seemed to be a suitable place that did not need too much work doing to it. It was big enough for her to set aside two rooms; one in which to work on her project and one to receive clients. The market seemed to be reasonably buoyant, and the estate agent said it would not be difficult to sell her flat. Lucy also tried to keep up her painting which she had enjoyed so much and which, after all had been the instigation for all that followed. Lucy went ahead with the project, certain in her own mind that she had done the right thing. After selling her flat she hoped that she would be able to raise enough money finally to have her long-awaited holiday.

Unusually, that morning a letter arrived from Richard. It was uncharacteristic of him to write again so quickly so she expected some bad news. She was, however, most agreeably surprised when she opened it to find that he and Sophie were planning to be married, albeit not for some time. He had enclosed a photograph of the two of them. Sophie certainly looked stunning with a mane of auburn curls and freckled skin. She was very happy for them but felt even keener to go out to stay with Richard so that she could meet Sophie. It would be nice to see them before their wedding which, after all, seemed to be some way off. They were both quite heavily committed one way and another, but she hoped that one day they would come back to settle in England. Richard had said that Sophie was Irish so perhaps they would settle in Ireland, but she supposed, like everyone else, they would have to follow their work. Lucy sat down straight away to write to Richard congratulating him on his engagement. She also told him about her prospective move and the studio. Lucy supposed that Richard had told his father and wondered what he thought about it.

***

Bob and Marjorie had found themselves a rather quaint cottage close to the South Devon coast and not too far from Bob's place of work. It was decided that Marjorie should not work. She needed to have as much rest as possible and was advised not to do anything too strenuous.

"Of course," Marjorie said to Bob one day when they were out on of their coastal walks that they enjoyed so much, "The odds are very much against me carrying this baby for nine months. I wonder, too, whether it will be healthy."

"Oh, don't think like that," Bob replied. "Be positive and what will be will be."

Bob decorated a small sunny room at the back of the cottage which they were going to make into the nursery.

"In any case, I'm not going to buy a lot of furniture and furnishings yet, nor clothes. I think that will be tempting providence."

She always had the fear in the back of her mind that the

event was not going to take place, and that to make preparations early would somehow influence the outcome, no matter how illogical this sounded. Bob decided not to tell Richard of this latest development. He had, after all, not taken too kindly to the fact that he had married Marjorie. This was understandable since as a result of her desertion, he had lost his playmates, although at the time he was too young to understand what was going on. Richard had written to him, telling him his news. This, Bob thought, had the makings of a complicated situation, so he hoped that their wedding would not take place for some time to come, allowing things to settle down.

As the time passed Marjorie became somewhat ambivalent about having another baby. Neither of them expected it, never mind planned for it. Marjorie's psychological condition was unstable before her marriage to Bob. Although the fresh start in a different part of the country initially seemed to work it did not completely heal the wounds. Her pregnancy did not do anything to help matters. She knew too that this would affect her children, if she ever found them, and Richard too. Marjorie suffered serious pangs of guilt about everything that had happened, but she took great care of herself, although sometimes she wished that she would lose the baby. She thought it would make life a good deal easier. What would have been a joy to her a few years ago, under normal circumstances, now felt like a punishment. Bob was worried about her. He wondered, too, how it could have happened since Marjorie had been adamant that she was not able to conceive again, and also taking her age into consideration. He could only hope that after the birth the outlook would change.

At twenty-eight weeks into her term, Marjorie began to experience bouts of low backache. Although intermittent the intervening time gradually became less until she was very worried. One night she awoke with abdominal cramps and contractions.

"Bob," she cried as she shook him to wake him up. "I think the baby's coming. Get a doctor quickly. I've terrible tummy pains and cramps."

Bob did not stop to fetch a doctor. He bundled her in his car and rushed her into hospital where, after a traumatic labour, she was delivered of a tiny baby girl who, looking very blue, was immediately placed in an incubator.

"I'm afraid I have to tell you both that the chances of your baby surviving are very slim," the obstetrician told them. "She is suffering from heart and lung problems which are affecting her breathing. I think you should prepare yourselves for the worst, you know. We will of course do everything in our power to save her, but you must also bear in mind, that because she has been starved of oxygen, even if she survives there's a strong possibility that she will be brain damaged."

Bob and Marjorie were devastated. They had her christened the next day. They called her Amy.

Despite all the efforts of the doctors and midwives they were unable to save Amy. It was a very distressing time. When the incubator was switched off, Marjorie was able to lift out the tiny body and give her the cuddle and kiss that she had been denied so far. "It's all my fault. Retribution for all my misdeeds and for wishing sometimes I'd lose the baby. Life seems so cruel and is not meant to work for me. I wish I could die too," she sobbed.

Bob was distraught and at a loss for words.

Bob wrote to congratulate his son on his engagement and wished them every happiness, something that at present seemed to be passing him by. In this same letter he told Richard about little Amy.

Chapter 10

The sun managed to peep through as the tiny white coffin, with its wreath of pale pink rosebuds, was carried from the church to the graveyard. A few friends accompanied Bob and Marjorie. Marjorie was pale and wan, clinging to Bob for support. A tear trickled down his cheek which made the moment even more poignant since he seldom showed any emotion.

Bob took Marjorie home. After the sad funeral of such a tiny baby, but a cherished life nevertheless, they had to try to pick up the pieces; try to lead a normal life again. Marjorie was inconsolable and, despite all the help that could be obtained from counselling and drugs, her mental state slowly deteriorated. Bob was beside himself with worry. He did not know what to do next. They went away for weekends and finally he took her on a ten-day cruise, but nothing made any difference. Marjorie continued to suffer from what can only be described as a guilt complex about all that had happened in her life and was clearly close to a nervous breakdown.

"I know this has been sent as a punishment for all the things that I've done wrong, particularly leaving my children when they were so young and vulnerable. I can see now how selfish it was of me to do such a thing," Marjorie cried to Bob on more than one occasion.

"Come on now you mustn't blame yourself for everything that's happened. You know how much you suffered at the hands of Tom. You were in an intolerable situation."

"Well, there were times when I thought it would be easier if the baby died. I wasn't sure whether I really wanted another child now or whether I would be able to cope. Nor did I know how Richard would take it or my other children if we were lucky enough to meet again. So I suppose I have reaped my just desserts. I just wish I were dead."

Bob, placid by nature, was beginning to get weary of listening to all this but was helpless as to know what to do. He thought it would be a good idea if she did some part-time work. It would perhaps take her mind off events if only for a short time each day. He managed to get her some employment in the office where he worked, but Marjorie was not happy about this. She did, however, give it a try and initially the dark clouds lifted a little. It was not very stimulating work, and after a few weeks she began to slip back into her old self again finding it increasingly difficult to get out of bed in the morning, so making herself late on many occasions. This was embarrassing for Bob who had been a pillar of support for her but was beginning to lose patience mainly because he did not really understand the condition. He thought that she had everything going for her.

One morning, when Marjorie was lingering in bed, the telephone rang. She managed to lean over to take the call. Most times she would have let the phone ring, never keen to answer. Somehow today she had an inkling that something was wrong.

"Hello. It's your brother here, Marjorie. I'm calling to let you know that Mother has been taken very ill and wonder whether you could come up to look after her for a while. She should go to hospital, but you know what she's like. She's adamant that she won't go, and I can't afford to get time off to stay at home."

The anxiety of all the latest events coupled with her ongoing chest problem had severely weakened her mother, although she had not been made aware of the whole story.

"I'm not feeling too good myself but the least I can do is to give it a try. I'll get Bob to drive me up as soon as possible." Bob took Marjorie home to her mother who was in bed. Marjorie seemed to rise to the challenge.

She could at last perhaps be useful. Marjorie helped her mother as much as she could, ensuring that she took the medication prescribed and cooking her tasty nourishing food. Her mother seemed to respond to this and each day, as she became a little stronger, she sat out of bed. Marjorie would sit with her and she enjoyed the short chats that they had together on these few occasions. At last Marjorie was able to open up a little. Her mother told her not to blame herself, much the same as everyone else, but talking did not erase the pain. Her mother also told her that a friend had managed to find a contact for the children. It was thought that they had been to Canada to look for her but had since returned. Marjorie always thought that to see her children again would be a dream come true but instead she was filled with dread and, deep down, feared rejection. The improvement in her mother was short lived. She had a relapse and her condition deteriorated rapidly. She eventually had to succumb to hospitalisation. This upset Marjorie and the guilt complex began to raise its ugly head again. Whatever she did went wrong.

***

Bob walked from the Coroner's Court somewhat relieved that there were not to be further inquiries. It had been established that Marjorie had taken her own life. In his mind he pieced together what had happened. Marjorie had left a note saying that she could not take any more. Her mother's death was the last straw and she thought that she was better out of everybody's way. Her mother was an elderly lady and in no way could Marjorie be blamed for this, but this was her perception. Marjorie's brother had found her slumped in a chair after she had returned from visiting the hospital one afternoon. There were a number of opened bottles of tablets by her side and an empty paracetamol packet had fallen to the floor. A half empty bottle of gin sat on the table and an empty glass, which smelt of gin had fallen to the floor. Marjorie's brother called the emergency services. They tried to resuscitate her without success. Bob concluded that she had hoarded tablets, when he thought she was picking up a little, while looking after her mother.

This was all a terrible blow to Bob especially as there was a letter for Marjorie which of course he had to open. It was from her children to say that they were on their way to visit. Bob began to wonder what he had done to deserve all this, but fortunately although very upset and sad at all the untimely events, he was level-headed and able to think rationally. The bottom had suddenly dropped out of his life once again. He thought it was probably much better if he lived on his own and did not enter into any more relationships. It did appear that no matter how firmly they seemed to be established, he could not make them last. He took some compassionate leave from his work and flew out to Australia. He thought a less stressful lifestyle for a couple of months and fresh company would help to ease the pain of the last three years, but at the moment he felt that he would never recover from all these untimely events. Bob felt raw inside, and something tugged and tugged at his heart. It was as though there was some demon that lingered always ready to snatch from him what little happiness he could find and neither had he anyone close in whom he could confide. Despite the death of his most recent wife Marjorie, fond feelings for Lucy remained, once buried deep in his heart but coming gradually closer to the surface.

Lucy established herself in her new home and studio. She continued to work by day in the art studio but took on work during the evenings at home. She placed advertisements in the local paper and very soon her business began to take off to the extent that she was no longer able to sustain full-time hours at the studio. She continued to do three mornings a week. This helped with the everyday expenses since she did not get paid for a commission until it was completed. Therefore, her income was quite irregular, depending on how much work she could get and when the final cheques would come through. She was pleased with her efforts. She could not help thinking what a turnaround there had been in her life, from ideas of going back to nursing, then waitressing and now this. Wow! She felt positively glowing.

Lucy was pleased that she had not jumped into a permanent relationship with Sandy but, nevertheless, he regularly crept into her thoughts. She wondered what had happened to him and whether he had returned from abroad, wherever that had been. She was also pleased that she had kept Pip at arm's length. She was unsure about him. He certainly was not the 'passionate sex at any price' character that Sandy had been. He was more down to earth, she thought. He seemed uncertain as to what or who he was really looking for. He had never divulged any of his inner feelings and he was difficult to read. She often thought about him, too, and wondered what he was doing.

It is strange how events happen and sometimes it seems as though thoughts provoke them. That afternoon, when Lucy returned from shopping at the supermarket, she picked up a local newspaper. Splashed over the front page was the photograph of a horrific crash. Who should be involved but Sandy! So, he was back then. Apparently, he had driven head on into a tree. It was suspected that he had been drinking but fortunately there was no one else involved and he was alone in the car. He had been rushed to the local hospital where he was put in intensive care on a life support machine. Lucy could feel her heart lurch and her pulse quicken. The feelings that had been thrust into the back of her subconscious began to push forward again. Her immediate reaction was to go and visit him. Then she wondered about Helen and how she would feel. She read on and further down the page it mentioned that he had been divorced from his wife some months beforehand.

Lucy plucked up courage to ring the hospital but was told that only family was allowed to visit and that he was comfortable. This incident had temporarily distracted Lucy, but she knew that she had too much to lose now by becoming involved. She would, however, give it a week and then ring again. If Sandy survived, he could at least say whether he would like her to visit him.

When Lucy arrived home the following day there was a message on her answerphone machine.

"We have seen your advertisement in the local paper, Mrs. Barber, and would like you to give us a call? We are a soft-furnishing company and would be interested to talk with you."

A soft-furnishing arm of a major store was to set up in the town and they would like her to quote a price for designing and fitting out the shop. Lucy rubbed her eyes. Was she dreaming? She rang back immediately and made an appointment to see the manager and the premises. This was exciting. For the time being, all thoughts of Sandy were pushed out of her mind. She very quickly made some suggestions as to what could be reasonably achieved within the budget, which she had to admit was generous. The manager liked her ideas, and she went home to put pencil to paper and sketch out some plans.

Lucy took her plans back to the manager. Together they chose the two most suitable and Lucy went home to price them up. This was a prestigious job for her and one that could only be good for her reputation. Her luck did seem to be in at the moment.

She heard from Richard who had written to tell her all about his father's very traumatic circumstances and how he had flown out to see them to try to recover a little. Bob was devastated and had talked at length to Richard who felt that inevitably there must be lasting scars, but time was a good healer. Apparently, he had also talked very fondly of Lucy.

Lucy was sad about the loss of the premature baby, and even more so over Marjorie's suicide. What an ordeal all this must have been for him. She really felt very sorry for him and wrote to offer her condolences:

'My Dear Bob

Richard has told me about your tragic losses. I don't know what to say. My heart goes out to you. I know it is of little comfort to you for me to say that time will heal the scars. We all know how deep they go and although the surface looks good underneath the wound remains.

It's good that you have joined Richard and Sophie in Australia and hope you find some comfort in their happiness. I understand that they are putting their plans on hold for the time being which is very thoughtful of them.

With love,

Lucy'

She told him that she had been planning to go out to see Richard, but she would wait now to see when the wedding was to be before she finalised her plans.

Lucy received a prompt reply from Bob, which was unusual as writing letters was not his strong point.

'My Dear Lucy

Thank you for your letter and condolences. It was kind of you to write. As you say I have to try to put the past behind me, but you will appreciate it is difficult.

Richard and Sophie are looking after me well and taking me out to different places of interest when their busy schedules allow them the time.

Australia is certainly a wonderful country and I think it

possible that I would like to settle here although it is early days to be thinking of that. There is much unfinished back home to sort out, besides which I don't know their long-term plans. I would not like to be so far away if they don't stay out here. I have taken up golf. It gives me a purpose for going out and also gives me a social life which has been sadly lacking in recent times. I'll probably stay for a month or so and then travel on to New Zealand. I don't wish to outstay my welcome.

Enough of me! I am pleased to hear that you are building up such a good business. You certainly seem to be getting as much work as you can cope with. Stick at it although I do not have to tell you that, do I?

Sophie is a delightful person. She and Richard make a good pair, he with his handsome looks and she with her beauty. She's from Ireland. Her father is a consultant in medicine, and I understand from Richard quite a wealthy one. She lost her mother a few years ago in a tragic accident so I am not alone with unhappy family events. I wish I had had someone with whom to share this holiday but that was not to be.

So sorry that you will not be coming out before the wedding, but I will look forward to seeing you whenever that may be.

Yours as ever,

Bob'

Lucy read and reread the letter which she felt was quite heart wrenching. She also detected some of the old feelings resurfacing. Time is a strange dimension. Could it be that they were about to be thrown together again? She certainly felt a great deal of emotion as she read the letter, but she was aware that she must not confuse sentiment and pity for something deeper.

Lucy pulled herself together and snapped out of her reverie. She could not let any of these events distract her from her work. After all, she had worked hard for this and some of her plans were about to come to fruition. She began to price up the two sets of plans that she and the manager had decided on. After a great deal of time and effort, she had the final figures ready. Lucy decided to hand-deliver them, for in that way she would be certain that they would be received and signed for. She carefully made duplicate copies. With a great deal of satisfaction, she finally sealed them in the large envelope, especially purchased, and tripped down to the store to deliver them.

As promised, within a week they had decided which of the two plans they were going ahead with, and Lucy was to call in at the shop. She was so elated that she felt as though she almost floated there that morning. She asked to see the manager.

"Hello, Mrs Barber. Do come in and take a seat. Now, we have decided on this second plan," said the manager, pulling a file from his filing cabinet, "but there are one or two fine details to be sorted."

"Right. I'm sure that won't be a problem," replied Lucy.

When she was returning from the store, who should she bump into but Sandy struggling to get along on two crutches.

"Fancy bumping into you of all people. How are you?" he asked.

"I'm fine, but more to the point what about yourself?"

"I'm on the mend now. Thank you for ringing the hospital by the way. It was good of you to inquire. I'm sure you didn't get far because they only divulge information to next of kin. They told me some time after."

He managed to balance closely enough to her to give her one of his very warm kisses. It was obvious to Lucy that she just had to listen to what Sandy wanted to say, and besides which, she was intrigued to know about his accident.

"Look, I can't stand here for long on these crutches so let's go into this café and have a coffee."

"OK, that sounds sensible. I have a little time to spare, besides which I would like to know what happened to you."

Lucy was horrified when she realised that it was six weeks since she had read about the crash. He had suffered from concussion, a number of lacerations, much bruising and two fractured femurs. Hence the crutches, but he was recovering well. He hoped it would not be too long before he could dispense with the plaster and the crutches.

"You've certainly made a miraculous recovery," said Lucy.

"Yeah, I suppose so. You know Helen eventually agreed to a

divorce which was made absolute just prior to my accident, so now I am on my own." He admitted that he had been drinking heavily as a result and that it was fortunate for him that no other vehicle had been involved. Sandy hoped that he would make a full recovery and he also hoped that Lucy would see him when he was a little more mobile.

"I would like that but at the moment I'm very busy. I have just accepted a contract to design the interior of the new soft-furnishing shop that's opening in the High Street. I can't afford to get involved in another relationship at this stage, but I'll be happy to meet you for the odd drink."

She gave Sandy a lift home to save him having a taxi and watched him hobble up the drive. The surrounding garden looked somewhat unkempt at the moment; the borders were full of weeds and the grass high. She supposed that with all that had taken place he had had little time to tend it. He put the key in the lock, and she waved him goodbye. To her amazement she did not feel the strength of feeling that she had for him previously. It did seem somewhat ironic that what should have been the perfect situation for them now seemed rather like a damp squib. Lucy remembered, of course, telling him that he should get himself sorted out before becoming involved with anyone else. She was unsure whether she really wanted to see him again. She wondered whether Bob's letter had had anything to do with it, and her mind was of course preoccupied with her new assignment.

Lucy was totally absorbed in her project, which kept her busy most of the day. She was conscious, however, that she must also think ahead and have something to continue with once it was completed. She also needed to get some money together for the impending wedding and her trip to Australia. How exciting things were. Her life certainly seemed to be taking a turn for the better. It would not be long before the shop would be opening so the manager was placing a full-page advertisement in the paper. This would be good news because she was to be one of the sponsors. She made the most of it, placing quite a large advert in a prominent position. She carefully set out the points of her business that she wished to emphasise and she beamed with pleasure at the finished design. 'Interior Design and Furnishings by Lucy Barber Ltd. The Woodlands Studio, Telephone...' She hoped it would bring her in a lot more business. Little did she guess just what the result would be.

***

Pip had arrived back from one of his many trips to Scotland. He decided to look around some of his old haunts. He remained in his caravan whilst he seriously looked around for a property that would be large enough to incorporate a studio. Having little to occupy him, one morning he decided to call in at the college on the off chance that there may be a vacancy for an art teacher, preferably part time. He really needed to have a small income but would like to continue his painting. As luck would have it, there was such a vacancy, but only temporarily while someone was on long-term sick leave. Pip returned to his van with, for a change, a little whistle and a spring in his step. It had poured with rain earlier and his clothes became very wet but as he walked back the rain had ceased and he felt the sun warm on his back. He thought he would even start to steam with heat. He had a quick look in some estate agents on the way but there did not appear to be anything suitable for him. He passed a newsagent's and picked up a local paper thinking that it was possible that something might be advertised, perhaps to let. As it had turned out to be such a beautiful afternoon, he thought he would go down to the riverbank. He could look at his paper and maybe do a little sketching.

Pip was astonished when he opened the centre page of the paper and saw a huge advertisement for the refurbished furniture shop, and there, in prime position: 'Interior Design and Furnishings by Lucy Barber.'

Lucy put down the telephone. This was something she had not expected from her advertisement. Her feelings were a mixture of pleasure, excitement and apprehension. The next morning, Pip duly arrived to see Lucy and have a cup of coffee. Never one for wearing his heart on his sleeve, Pip took Lucy's hand and shook it warmly. Such a contrast, she thought, to her latest encounter with Sandy.

"Fine place you have here," Pip volunteered as he cast his

eye around the room.

"It suits me well," replied Lucy. "You see I have a studio also, with a reception area."

"Do you still have time to do some painting?" asked Pip. "And by the way I stopped at a pub on my way to Scotland and sure enough there were paintings by Lucy Barber. Who would have thought it, but then I always knew there was some undeveloped talent there."

"Oh, yes they sold quite a lot for me," answered Lucy. "I went up to visit an old friend and that's how it all came about," answered Lucy. "Strange how things turn out."

Chapter 11

Pip and Lucy talked until it was almost lunch time. It had, after all, been some time since they had seen each other and inevitably there was a great deal of news to impart. Pip told Lucy that he had a temporary post at the college again. This seemed to please her. He also told her that he was looking to buy a house large enough to incorporate a studio with some of the money that his mother had left him. Lucy thought this was the right course of action and offered to help him if she could, since she had gained quite a lot of experience of appraising property over the last year.

"It's a beautiful day and a shame to be indoors," said Lucy. "How about taking a few sandwiches to eat down by the river? It won't take a moment for me to make some."

"That's a good idea. While you make the sandwiches, I'll nip down the road and buy some cold drinks."

Pip and Lucy made their way to the riverbank. Lucy grabbed a couple of umbrellas.

"The sun is shining now, but you can't be too certain what the weather will do, and they did forecast showers," she said as they left the house. They walked along the bank. The same walk exactly that Lucy had taken some four or five years or more ago when she first ran into Pip. It was a crossing of paths that was to change the course of her life, which at present was looking pretty good. She could not help thinking how lucky she had been compared with the traumatic events that Bob had had to endure, the latest of which still hung over her like a black cloud. She could not understand why she should be so deeply affected by this. Sometimes it almost felt as though it had happened to her.

"You have gone very pensive all at once," remarked Pip. "Is something bothering you?"

"As a matter of fact, yes," replied Lucy and she proceeded to relate the whole sorry story to Pip who listened attentively.

"Well," he answered, "I have never told anyone else this, but I had an experience which shattered me and changed me as a person."

Pip related to Lucy all about the accident with his fiancée and how, since his mother died, he was really only just coming to terms with it.

"We all think that such experiences set us apart from everybody else. I think they change us, you know. Although they're traumatic at the time, it is possible that they give us a different perspective on life and can sometimes make us stronger people. More often than not, it's possible to use them positively once the grieving has passed and we pick out the wood from the trees. It really took the loss of my mother to bring me to my senses, finally heeding what she had said to me on more than one occasion."

Lucy listened intently to what Pip had to say. He had not only been a good listener but also appeared to be intuitive with a balanced and sensible approach to life. They walked on to the clearing where the artists usually set out their canvasses and found a bench on which to sit and eat their sandwiches. As usual, there was plenty of wildlife to watch. Lucy was surprised at how knowledgeable Pip was about all the birds. They sat in silence for some time just drinking in all the pleasures of the countryside. The sun, which had felt warm on them until now, was gradually being eclipsed by a large black cloud.

"It looks as though we're going to be caught in a storm if we're not careful. There's a big black cloud hovering up there. I think we'd better make tracks while the going's good," said Lucy "Besides which, I have a great deal of work to do."

"I think that's probably right. I need to go back and have another scour through the paper to see what I can find. Will I see you again?" asked Pip.

"Oh yes, I'd like that very much," replied Lucy.

"I'll give you a ring then next week sometime."

When Lucy arrived home, she reflected on her walk with Pip. She thought that despite the length of time since she had seen him, he did not seem to have aged that much. Perhaps this was because he had trimmed his beard and tidied up his hair. She wondered whether they would see each other again. She certainly hoped so, for she was beginning to warm to him very much. This was the opposite effect that Sandy had had on her having not seen him for a considerable length of time. She was beginning to think Sandy was not the right person for her, if indeed she really wanted another commitment.

It was Wednesday morning, the telephone rang and Lucy rushed to answer thinking it might be more business.

"Hello, Lucy Barber Interior Designs," she answered.

"Hi there!" It was Pip's voice, so he was as good as his word. "Would you like to come out to dinner with me tomorrow evening," he asked. "I thought we could go to the 'Turnpike'. I've heard good reports about it," Pip continued.

"That sounds like a really good idea. Of course I'd love to come!"

"About seven o'clock then."

"Yes, that'll give me plenty of time," replied Lucy.

Lucy allowed herself to feel just a tiny bit excited about this but, nevertheless, she had some reservations. Would this turn into more of a commitment than just a drink in a pub or a café? Oh well, she thought, no harm can be done just this once. Since Pip had told her about his accident, she had wondered why he had had so much to drink that evening. Was it just a one-off occasion or was he prone to this? She was left wondering what predisposed this situation since he and Angela were supposedly happy and about to be married. Was there something about him of which she was unaware? A little nagging doubt crept into the back of her mind. Despite this niggle, the evening went ahead, and Lucy had to admit that she did enjoy Pip's company and, perhaps, she was being unduly wary about him. She did notice though that he did not drink any alcohol. They went on to see each other on a regular basis. Pip continued to look around for his house but was not so fortunate as Lucy had been.

"I have an idea," said Lucy one day when they were out for a walk. "My studio is large enough for two people to work in so why not join me until you can find something more suitable. I'll let you have it for a modest rent. It'll be beneficial to us both. It'll give you somewhere to get started and me a little extra income."

"I could look after the reception area for you and take the calls when you are out on business."

It was agreed that this should commence immediately. Pip

moved his materials round and started painting. The new arrangement seemed to be working very well until one evening when Lucy returned feeling rather tired and stressed from a meeting to find Pip still in the studio.

"Oh, I didn't expect to see you still here," called Lucy as she entered the studio.

"You're working later than usual tonight Pip," said Lucy.

"Well, to tell the truth I'm getting a bit behind with the work for the exhibition next month so I thought an extra hour or so would help me get back on track."

This was partly the reason, but Pip had another idea. He had realised that since spending more time closer to Lucy it was becoming increasingly difficult to disguise his feelings for her, which were more than just friendship. So far, his tentative approaches had not been reciprocated. They had dined out on several occasions, taken walks along the river and spent endless time discussing paintings and art work, yet he was no closer to her.

Pip looked nervously at the clock ticking away the minutes. It was approaching seven o'clock. The doorbell rang and although he was expecting it Pip was startled.

"Whoever can this be? I'm not expecting anyone. Are you?" said Lucy in surprise.

"Well as a matter of fact I am. Let me answer the door then I'll explain," replied Pip.

Lucy went into her living room and noticed that the table was set for two. She was puzzled and wondered what was going on.

"Thanks," she heard Pip say as he took a package with a distinct whiff of curry from the delivery man.

Coming into the room he explained that he had taken the liberty of ordering them a take-away, as a surprise. He had something rather special to say to her. He thought it would be cosier to talk at home.

"Well it's certainly a surprise. I'm very tired this evening and in no mood for either being entertained or entertaining.

I'll also point out, this is my home not yours. I've had a particularly trying day and just wanted some time to myself."

Pip looked crestfallen. He had never heard Lucy speak like this. She was usually so calm and considerate.

"Oh well if that's the way you feel, I'll leave your meal and take mine home. I'm so sorry to hear that you've had such a bad time. This was meant to give us a bit of cheer nearing the end of a busy week but I've no desire to stress you further, far from it, and neither is it the time to talk to you as I'd hoped," answered Pip in his usual self-deprecating manner.

"No need to leave anything for me. I've eaten. James, a business associate, took me out to lunch, rather late, so I've no room for curry."

As Pip made ready to leave, Lucy did begin to feel rather ashamed of herself.

"Sorry, Pip, for being so churlish. I know this was meant as a kindness. Give me some time and I'll have a shower. By then I'll feel more rested and will enjoy a small helping of curry."

Lucy made her way upstairs, planting each foot heavily, as though she was climbing a mountain. Pip turned and left very quietly without saying goodbye. He was hurting inside. He felt a burning searing pain surge through him. He didn't go straight back to his van but took a walk along the river. When he reached the bridge, through the low rays of the setting sun, he stood looking into the water as it flowed silently, stealthily, with gentle ripples in contrast to Pip's churning inside. A thought flashed through his mind that this gentle water could end it all for him. He was about to make a decisive move, when a car came hurtling down the road and pulled up with a screech of brakes as a deer ran across its path, dazzled by the head-lights. There was a loud thud. Pip turned, almost losing his footing, as he was, fleetingly, thrown back to that devastating moment in his life. He was stunned. A tall, sandy-haired fellow, jumped out of the car to assess the damage to his vehicle and to see whether he had killed or injured the animal. As he came into focus, Pip recognised Sandy. Lucy had talked a lot about him and he remembered his face from their journey on the train. The deer lay in a sad, bloody heap in the middle of the road.

"Damn, poor thing," he muttered under his breath.

Sandy looked up to see this wan individual, seemingly

shocked by what had happened.

"Poor thing didn't have a chance," called Sandy as he walked towards Pip.

As he approached Pip, Sandy judged by the expression on his face that it was more than the deer that had upset Pip.

Sandy said in a soft voice as he reached him, "Can I be of any help. Have you lost your way? Oh, I believe it's Pip. Am I right?"

"Yes it is. I'm OK thanks. Just feeling a bit low, that's all."

"I'm on my way home but thought I would call in for a drink and a sandwich at the pub. How about you join me. A drink and a chat will help to cheer you up I'm sure. I'll have to call in at the police station on the way to report this accident. I could do with a bit of moral support."

Pip could not refuse.

Sandy noticed his pallor and trembling hands. They reported the deer incident and went on to the pub. After a brandy, Pip began to relax a little.

"I'll run you home. I don't know about you but I'm feeling a bit shaken up."

Sandy returned by a long route to allow Pip to settle. When they reached Pip's van Sandy asked Pip if he could make him a strong coffee before he left. Pip agreed, realising that he had reached rock-bottom.

Before Sandy left he had the drift of what had happened and Pip had also told him about Angela's death and how he reproached himself for it. Sandy suggested that Pip should take a long break and seek some help.

After a shower Lucy eventually went downstairs, feeling more refreshed. She called out to Pip but there was no answer. She looked around and deduced that he must have left. Now she really did feel worried and ashamed. It was not in her nature to be so thankless but she was tired after a day of phone calls and appointments to fulfil. She also had a large contract on her books, with a deadline. She was beginning to wonder whether she had taken on too much. Then she thought it was probably nothing more than a night's sleep would put right. She had no idea what Pip wanted to say and neither was she interested. It could surely wait. The evening was hers but at what cost?

The next morning Pip did not come to the studio at his normal time and neither was he answering the phone. Lucy had an engagement to keep and would be away all day. She slowly turned the key in the lock, feeling somewhat uneasy, as she left that morning.

Pip, although still traumatised, had managed to pull himself together after Sandy left and did some thinking. He was probably right; a change of surroundings would be good for him. After a restless night he hastily packed his bags and knowing Lucy would not be in, called to pick up his gear. He bought a bouquet of flowers, which he left on the table with a simple thank you note. He carefully locked the door and posted the key through the letterbox. He drove off, headed for his old home village. He would try to pick up some old ties; not spend so much time alone, dwelling on the situation. As he drove through the countryside Pip realised that the death of the deer had saved his life. He vowed to himself from then on to make more of it.

***

"Thank you, son, for a wonderful holiday. It did help to take my mind off recent events quite a lot," said Bob as he gave Richard a big hug and slap on the back.

"Take care, Dad, and have a safe journey," replied Richard as Bob made his way to the departure lounge and turned to give Richard one last wave. Bob was going to spend a few weeks in New Zealand before returning to the UK. Richard was not usually moved by such farewells, but today he did feel more than a little sad. It was one of those really hot days when all you wanted to do was to chill out by the pool, but Richard decided not to go home right away. He had taken the day off from his work, but nevertheless did not wish to spend the day alone. Sophie had not been able to take time off, so he had to while away the day. It was almost lunch time and what better way than to go to a bar have something to eat and a long cool drink. He would probably meet up with some pals and this would take his mind off the departure of his father.

Richard would not admit to being affected by the traumatic experiences of his father, but he was indeed. Deeply so. He had been concerned not only at his father's loss of weight and rapidly receding hair, but also at his quiet and withdrawn manner. This was so unlike him. However, he had seemed considerably brighter when he left so perhaps the break and the opportunity to talk to someone close had made a little difference. He hoped that he would not slip back once on his own again. He promised to keep in close contact with his father and would let him know all about the wedding plans once they had decided on a date. The wedding would of course be in Sophie's home village.

Richard felt though that talking too much now about what should be a happy time was a little insensitive. Sophie agreed, so they decided to put off any further arrangements for at least another three months. This would perhaps give all concerned a little more time to come to terms with the recent traumas. There was the question of getting parents to meet one another, and he also had to decide how much of his father's situation he should disclose to her father. To date, he had only been told of Bob and Lucy's divorce. Bob had been quite open about everything to Sophie, but Richard could not help feeling a little apprehensive about telling Patrick all that had taken place as, indeed, was Sophie. Religion played a prominent part in his life and Sophie knew he liked to observe the conventions. However, by the same token, he was obviously a well-educated person and a man of the world. His profession and research work had brought him in touch with people from all backgrounds and those who had faced similar problems. Sophie also knew how much she meant to him. She was also aware that he would not wish anything to come between them and, although he would voice a true opinion, he would not stand in her way, even if he did not approve. Richard and Sophie both decided that it was Richard's character that was important and not what had happened to other members of the family. For the time being, then, they left matters as they stood.

***

As the last patient left his consulting room, Patrick picked up his phone and asked his secretary to look at his future appointments to see whether there was a reasonable gap later in the year or where at least they could create one by rearranging some of the appointments. Patrick was beginning to feel that it was time he met Richard. He was, after all, hoping to marry his daughter and he could not expect Richard and Sophie to take time off to come home before their wedding. September seemed to be a good month, so Patrick telephoned Sophie to say that he was coming out in September. It would serve as his annual holiday and also afford him the opportunity to meet Richard. This pleased Sophie immensely as she wanted to show off Richard to her father. She knew he was a difficult person to please but felt that he would like Richard. There was always a hint of 'I hope you are doing the right thing' in his voice when he spoke to her on the telephone. Typical, Sophie thought, of a doting father. The date was agreed, and Patrick set about finding a suitable flight. He only knew a little of Richard's background and was anxious to see him to learn more.

Sophie and Richard agreed that it would be best to tell her father the whole story now that some time had elapsed, so the real reason for Bob's visit would be revealed. They were unsure how he would receive this. Patrick also expressed a wish to meet Lucy but thought that this would be better after his trip to Australia.

One evening over their dinner, Sophie and Richard decided that the best time for their wedding would be in early June of the following year. This would give everyone back home ample time to prepare. They would of course have to go over a few weeks prior to this in order for them to check that everything was in order and also to meet the requirements of the Church. So, this was all set.

Patrick was stifled by the suddenness of the heat coming from the tarmac as it hit him when he stepped off the plane. It was not long before Sophie was in his arms. He was so pleased to see her. She introduced Richard to whom he took an instant liking. He and Sophie had so much to talk about. Patrick had booked into a hotel. This would be better since he did not wish Richard and Sophie to entertain him all the time. They had their work and they had also not long ago had Bob with them. He had also one or two colleagues, who were now working out there, that he wished to look up and with whom to discuss some research papers. Patrick asked how Bob had enjoyed his stay and what he was doing. This seemed a good time to let him know of all the sad events that had taken place. Patrick was, indeed, deeply sorry about all of this and understood why Bob needed to take a long break. Patrick also expressed a desire to meet both his parents and he conceded that this would be better done on separate occasions. Richard assured him that both parents were also keen to meet him. They confirmed that the wedding would take place in June of the following year. Patrick seemed to be happy about this. He made it clear that it would be a Catholic wedding and that any children would have to be brought up in that faith. Before he left, he was careful to take contact numbers and addresses for both Bob and Lucy.

Patrick, back home now, thought that he had better approach Lucy about meeting her. He thought the best time would be when he was next in London. Maybe Lucy would meet him for lunch one day. They could then perhaps do a little sight-seeing. Somehow, he worried about Bob's troubled situation. He thought he must be an extremely unhappy person. Patrick had found Richard to be such a personable and clever young man but deep down he wondered how these traumatic family events had affected him, as they surely must have in some way. He hoped that they would not have any lasting effect on a long-term relationship. Certainly, at the moment, Richard seemed to be quite philosophical about it all but sometimes these effects rear their ugly heads much later. While in Australia he did take Sophie to one side and voiced some concerns. She was certain that everything would be fine, and, after all, it was Richard she was to marry and not the family.

Meanwhile Lucy received a letter from Bob. It was sometime since he had returned but he said that he would like to see her to have a chat and to let her know all about his trip. Strangely, Lucy felt a frisson of excitement.

Chapter 12

Lucy was surprised to find that Pip's sudden departure had affected her so adversely. She had to admit that she missed him a lot; his gentle chatter, always ready to lend an ear, give helpful suggestions. She wondered, on more than one occasion, why she had become so irritated with his presence. After all, he had been a good companion, soulmate and also her confidant. He had taught her, unstintingly, to paint and develop her untapped talent. She owed him a debt of gratitude, for it was his patient teaching that had allowed her to create a successful business, which had ultimately provided her much yearned for independence.

It saddened Lucy to think that it was her foolish and selfish behaviour that had led to Pip's departure and the loss of a good friendship. A friendship like they had had relied on giving, but apart from allowing Pip the use of her studio, she recognised now, too late, how little her contribution had been. There was nothing she could do to make amends. It appeared that Pip had left the area without disclosing his whereabouts to anyone.

Lucy had bumped into Sandy one afternoon, when he told her about the incident with the deer. He told her he had found Pip in a very sorry state but had managed to help him get a grip of himself, which presumably had led to his decision to make a clean break, to have a fresh start. Sandy had revealed a considerate and compassionate side to his nature which, until now, he had kept well hidden. He had been Pip's life-line, for which she was truly thankful.

Lucy also thought that it was probably about time that she had another short break. Perhaps she could go up to see Mary, so she gave her a call.

"Hello there, Mary. It's Lucy here."

"What a lovely surprise. Are you coming up to see us then?"

"I'd love that if you can manage it. I really do feel that I need a break and I have lots to tell you."

Mary, as always, was pleased to hear from Lucy so it was arranged that she should go up for a long weekend.

On her arrival they sat out in the new conservatory enjoying the dying rays of the evening sun. As usual, Malcolm was working late. Lucy told Mary all about Richard and Sophie and how excited she was over the wedding, also the possibility of her seeing them before it took place. Mary remembered, of course, how Lucy had postponed this trip while she finished her course at the college.

"You certainly seem to be having a very busy time. Much more exciting than me. All I seem to do is to wait for Malcolm to return from work and take Buster for walks," replied Mary. With that Buster cocked his head to one side and pricked up his ears.

"All right, we'll take you out very shortly," Mary said.

"There's much more to tell you but it'll take me some time," explained Lucy.

"Well, we'll take the dog along the beach first and then we can talk in peace when we return," answered Mary. "I've been meaning to ask you about some fellow who called at the local pub and said that he knew you. He was on his way to Scotland. He recognised your name on the paintings that they hung for you."

"Oh yes, thereby hangs a tale. It's a long story," Lucy began. "He was the artistic kind of bohemian chap that I first saw on the train, when I returned from London. You remember? When I went down for an interview."

"Ah, there was someone else too wasn't there?" asked Mary.

"Yes, that was Sandy. Pip was the artist who introduced me to painting, and you could say who is responsible in a way for my life as it is now. He is also partly the reason why I needed a break," went on Lucy.

Mary, looking quizzical, said, "Tell me about it."

"There was something I didn't quite understand about him. I returned from work one evening, after a stressful day, expecting to have some time on my own, to find that he had arranged a take-away meal for us both. He also said he needed to talk to me. Goodness knows what that was all about. I told him I thought he was taking a liberty and to cut a long story short it led to his departure. I think I reacted irrationally but I was so tired, and a bit tetchy, I suppose. I do miss him. After Angela's death, Pip found forging new relationships difficult. However, reading between the lines, I'm pretty sure his friendship had grown into something deeper for me, but he wasn't able to express those feelings. Unintentionally, I piled on the stress."

Lucy told Mary about the incident with the deer and how Sandy had come to his rescue that evening.

Mary was quite taken aback by this exposition replying, " Oh, how very sad. Well, at least you know he received help and from Sandy of all people. You must put it behind you now, and concentrate on your business."

"You're lucky, Mary, that you still have your husband. Meeting someone after a divorce is a tricky business, after you've been married and had a child. When you're young you seem to grow together. That can't happen when you're older. There always seem to be so many pitfalls. You don't appreciate how much, nor what has happened in the past which is bound to have an effect on any future partnership. I suppose, in some cases, you never find out what has made a potential partner tick. It pays to be wary and, sadly, not so trusting later on in life," mused Lucy.

"Do you ever hear from Bob now," asked Mary. "With the wedding coming up, I suppose you're bound to have some contact."

"Strange you should ask about Bob. There's another long, sad tale to tell," replied Lucy.

Lucy proceeded to tell Mary all about the traumas that Bob had experienced and how worried Richard was about him.

"Not only that, but it does appear to have had a profound effect on me too, which I can't understand. In some ways I suppose I feel a bit responsible because if we hadn't split up, none of this would've happened. Besides, I have to say, I still have some affection for him, but I'm not sure whether it's pity or lingering love. To complicate matters, it seems he wants to see me. I wonder why? He wrote to me soon after he returned from Australia, said he thought it'd be a good idea to re-acquaint ourselves before the wedding, sooner rather than later."

"That's understandable I suppose, but Lucy, please be careful. I told you this when you went down to London and look what happened! Don't get into anything that you're likely to regret afterwards."

"I know, but you must also remember the positive things that came as a result," replied Lucy. "I think Bob is too broken to be too much of a threat."

"Well, mind you don't get roped in to looking after him!"

"No chance!" laughed Lucy. "I also have to meet Sophie's father at some point."

"From what you've told me about him I don't anticipate any problems there."

"I have to try to fit in a trip to Australia too. I'm so looking forward to it. It's something that I've always wanted to do and now, if I'm careful, it just seems possible as long as nothing goes wrong out there with them. You never know!" said Lucy.

"You do seem to have problems with all your suitors," laughed Mary. "How many are there in the frame now? This is all reminiscent of those heady student days and Patrick. The times you were late back and had to climb through your window. What about the night you came tumbling in on top of me mistaking my window for yours. Gosh... We wouldn't get away with those pranks, today.

The fun helped us through the serious situations though."

"Yes I suppose so. And yes, I certainly do remember Patrick. It took me a long time to get over him. In fact, to tell the truth I don't think I ever have. No one's ever come up to him or at least to my memory of him. In fact, I've often thought recently that I married on the rebound. My mother always said that's what she did and never really knew what she meant until now."

"Oh well. I think that's an excuse," retorted Mary.

Lucy left 'Three Chimneys' on Monday morning feeling much refreshed after a few nights away. It's surprising, she thought to herself, what a difference it makes when you can talk things over with someone you trust. It had taken her sometime to calm her nerves and to settle herself down after the incident. Maybe in a week or two she would be ready to face Bob. It would be good to get some first-hand information about Richard and Sophie, and also to see where they lived. At the moment, they lived in different places. Lucy was not sure if this was purely to do with their places of work or whether Sophie's father would not approve of them living together or indeed perhaps they had just chosen not to. It really did not matter at this stage.

***

Bob was waiting for Lucy on the concourse under the clock at Southampton railway station, a half-way meeting place. It was a cold grey day, as days so often seemed to be. Bob was wearing an overcoat and scarf, which was most unusual for him, so he must be feeling the cold, thought Lucy. He greeted her with a very warm hug. He looked so wan. The pain and anguish of the latest events were etched in his face.

"It's good to see you. I'm so pleased that you were able to come. I've booked two rooms at the George's Hotel. We should be comfortable there."

"That rather special" replied Lucy.

"Nothing but the best."

He hasn't changed in that respect, thought Lucy, but she was very thankful to be ushered into a waiting taxi and whisked off somewhere for a warming drink. Lucy felt comfortable with Bob, which surprised her. She had anticipated that this meeting might be difficult, but she felt quite at ease. She was even more confused now.

"Well, tell me all about Australia and how you found Sophie and Richard," Lucy asked eagerly. "I'm longing to go out to see them."

"You'll enjoy it out there I'm sure," answered Bob as he pushed the remainder of his hair from his eyes. They were quite pale, and watery. She noticed, too, a bluish tinge around his mouth. She wondered how well he really was, despite his assertion of good health.

"I didn't really want to come back and I'll consider returning once Sophie and Richard are married. I couldn't stay because I'll have to work my notice and of course pack up. I don't wish to keep the cottage," continued Bob.

"It sounds like a good idea, but tell me about Richard."

"Richard looks well and is progressing in his work. He'll have told you about his latest promotion. Sophie is a stunner. She has the most beautiful auburn hair and green eyes. She is also a very clever girl, very ambitious too. Following in her father's footsteps I understand. Have you met him yet?"

"No, not yet, but I hope to do so in the near future."

"I believe after the wedding, initially they'll stay in Richard's apartment. It's fairly central. The last I heard was that they are to be married in early June."

That evening, over dinner, Bob poured his heart out to Lucy. It was obvious that it was going to take him a long time to recover from the emotional roller coaster that he had suffered over the last two or three years. Lucy felt his pain. She worried, too, that it was having an effect on his general health. He really did not seem to have a firm idea of what he wanted to do or where he was going. She did get the impression that he would like a reconciliation. Maybe even a trial at getting together again, but Lucy dismissed this in her own mind as an impossible outcome. The weekend passed quickly, and Lucy had to admit that she had enjoyed it a great deal more than she had expected. They agreed to see each other again.

"Next time," Lucy suggested, "perhaps you would like to stay with me and then I can show you my studio and paintings."

"I would like that very much. Let's make it soon."

Bob said that he would be in touch with her shortly. They parted on far more amicable terms than they had left one another before.

Lucy concentrated on her work for the next few weeks, pushing the past events into the back of her mind. Every now and again her thoughts drifted to Bob. Her heart really went out to him. Sandy rang her from time to time. She did look forward to his calls, but she was very careful not to let this relationship resurface although she had to admit that she was beginning to feel that very strong attraction for him again. It just would not go away. She understood from Sandy that Pip had returned to the village where his parents had last lived, and was receiving treatment from a psychiatrist. This was a good thing as far as Lucy was concerned, because she was afraid that she might bump into him at any time. In fact, Sandy thought that Pip might eventually move away altogether.

Sandy was beginning to feel that he was getting on to a

stronger footing with Lucy. He appreciated how much her business meant to her, and also that she was probably not in the right frame of mind for him to make any overtures to her at this time. He remained very attracted to her and hoped that he could revive the dying embers of that first passion and make them burn brightly once more. He'd try.

Lucy arrived home one evening after visiting some clients. She was tired so she kicked off her shoes, made herself a drink, put on her favourite country album, sat with her feet up and opened her mail. She tossed most of it to one side, mainly brown envelopes which meant bills, and she was not in the mood to be looking at those now. Then, right at the bottom of the pile she noticed an envelope of expensive stationery, with an Irish stamp addressed in long-hand. The handwriting looked vaguely familiar. She was puzzled. She hurriedly opened it and to her surprise it was from Sophie's father. So why should the handwriting seem familiar? She read the letter, which was an invitation to see him in London one weekend when he was over. He thought that in view of the pending wedding, they should at least be acquainted. Underneath his signature he had written his name in full. She could not believe it. His surname was O'Connell. This, she remembered, was the name of the student that she had met some thirty years ago whilst doing her nursing training. The young trainee doctor with whom she had fallen so madly in love and for whom she still carried a torch. Could it possibly be the same person? He had been Irish, qualified in medicine and with the same name! Sophie's name, too. She had not made any connection with this at the time Richard had told her. Her heart lurched. It was surely too much of a coincidence to be the same Patrick. She dismissed the idea instantly, trying not to allow herself to be too carried away. Nevertheless, the writing looked familiar, as she cast her mind back to those letters that she had had to burn, always beautifully crafted, that had always haunted her; the love that had never been allowed to blossom; the love she thought could have been the cause of, or at least contributed to, her troubled marriage.

Lucy accepted the invitation. They agreed on a time in about six weeks. They were to meet in London and to have lunch after which they would do a little sightseeing. Lucy was really looking forward to this but at the same time she felt mildly apprehensive. She dared not mention her thoughts to anyone for fear of being wrong. Anyway, Patrick had probably forgotten all about her. He had obviously had a very busy life and travelled widely. How strange that this should arise at the same time that she suspected Bob would like to have another try at living together. Lucy thought that this was out of the question. She had too much to lose now, and there was a lifetime of events to bridge. She did not wish to risk things going wrong a second time, besides which she was happy to be on her own at the moment. She hardly dared ask herself how she would feel if Patrick turned out to be the Patrick of her dreams. Then of course, there was Sandy. She realised that he, too, was longing to pick up their relationship again. He was always in the equation.

Lucy certainly did not have an easy life. Her peace was to be shattered once again. A telephone call from Richard:

"Hello, Mum."

"Hello, Richard. What a lovely surprise to hear your voice but is something wrong? You don't often call. You sound very worried." She sensed something urgent in Richard's tone.

"I'm afraid that I'm the bearer of very sad news. Dad had a massive heart attack and he died before reaching the hospital."

Lucy was devastated but she had remembered what a bluish tinge he had when she had seen him and how ill he looked. Really, she should not have been surprised. She was more upset than she thought she should be at such news sad though it was. Richard was coming home to arrange the funeral and organise the estate of which he was the sole beneficiary. She immediately contacted Patrick to let him know that their plans would have to be postponed temporarily. This was a bitter disappointment to Lucy but a situation that could not be avoided.

Richard arrived very shortly afterwards. He had to go to the West country where his father had moved with Marjorie; to the cottage where all those dreams for the future had finally been shattered. Lucy went down to help him for a few days and to attend the funeral.

Now seemed to be the right time for Lucy to visit Australia

for three or four weeks. It would give her time to settle her thoughts, away from everything and everyone that was familiar. She had confided in Richard about Sandy and Pip. She told him what she thought his father's feelings had been towards her.

Richard was a bit mystified, finding it all rather difficult to comprehend. He had no idea that his mother was such a complex character.

"You certainly lead a complicated life. What are your long-term plans? Would you like to be married again?"

"To tell you the truth, Richard, I'm too shaken up at present to make any forward plans. I would like to see you happily married and settled first."

Richard had to return to his work as soon as possible. He left the winding up of his late father's estate in the hands of his solicitor. Lucy followed in three weeks when she was able to leave her projects and potential clients. She also had to sort out a wardrobe. It was ages since she had bought herself any new clothes. She had had so little time for herself lately. She did look forward to her trip, but it was tinged with a great deal of sadness. She wondered whether she would ever recover from it even though she had not been directly involved. Lucy felt for Richard too. He said very little, but he had been very fond of his father despite their uneasy relationship when he was a child. Lucy knew that he had shared his grief. He had never understood why his parents' marriage went so badly wrong. He had always hoped that, somehow, they would patch things up and get together again.

Richard and Sophie both went to meet Lucy. Richard introduced his mother. She caught hold of Sophie's hand, at the same time giving her an affectionate hug and kiss.

It was of course the first time that she had seen Sophie. She certainly lived up to reports and photographs. She was not just photogenic.

"I am so pleased to have met you at last. You look positively blooming."

They drove home, all chatting excitedly.

"You'll be looking forward to your wedding and getting excited no doubt. How are the plans progressing?" asked Lucy.

"Well, there have been so many traumatic events recently that really the edge has been taken off the excitement for the time being," answered Sophie."

"I've no doubt it'll return after a while. You've plenty of time."

"Yes, I suppose so. We really don't want to postpone it again."

They gave Lucy a wonderful time. It was a holiday that she would never forget. It really was a trip of a lifetime. Like all good things, and in particular holidays, it seemed to be over in a flash. They had packed so much into it.

As Lucy disembarked from the long-haul flight, the cold late Autumn air and a biting wind caught her with a vengeance. What a contrast! Whilst she waited, travel weary and somewhat dishevelled, for her luggage to appear on the carousel, she could not help wondering what fate held in store for her now. Her purpose was to settle back into a work routine, for at last, she had achieved the main objective in her life, to become self-sufficient and a successful business person. There would be some tight deadlines to meet after a three-week break. There was also the weekend to fit in to meet Patrick.

Patrick was to meet Lucy off her train at Waterloo. They were each to wear a white carnation. They also exchanged recent photographs. When Patrick received the photograph of Lucy, he was amazed to find that her face was so familiar. Lucy had said nothing to him about her thoughts in case she was wrong. It had taken her a long time to decide what to wear. She was unsure whether to look smart or casual. She decided in the end on a navy-blue suit with a pale blue blouse. She packed casual clothes for sightseeing and two evening dresses. It felt as though she was going on her first date. Why? As the train approached the platform, Lucy felt a shiver run up her spine and she went a little cold. It was reminiscent of the day she went down for that fateful interview. She hoped that the results of this journey would not be as catastrophic as the last. As she alighted from the train, there he was, this attractive fellow, a little more corpulent, curly haired, albeit grey now, whom she remembered from all those years ago, wearing a white carnation. The thoughts she had tried hard to suppress were really true. Would he remember her, she wondered? He took one look and gasped.

"Good heavens, it's Lucy. I don't believe it," he exclaimed as he put his arms around her giving her a very affectionate hug. "This can't be true! I've often thought about you but never in my wildest dreams did I imagine I'd ever see you again."

Lucy almost collapsed in his arms. Despite everything that had gone before, that old feeling had returned. They had so much to talk about over lunch and beyond; old times, marriages, births, deaths and divorce and now another wedding. Patrick had decided that it would be more enjoyable to spend the weekend in Stratford and had booked rooms in a country hotel called The Granary. It was reminiscent of the Old Mill where they had said their last goodbye.

"This is heavenly," whispered Lucy, almost afraid to speak for fear of breaking the magic.

"I thought you would like this," answered Patrick. After a late evening exchanging their experiences and adventures, Lucy went to bed in a daze. This was the stuff of fairy tales. She had to pinch herself to make sure that she was not dreaming.

The weekend passed so quickly. They did some sightseeing, visiting Shakespeare's house and Anne Hathaway's cottage. In the evening they enjoyed a production of 'As you Like It' at The Royal Shakespeare Theatre. Patrick was so kind and attentive to her every need.

Over their last dinner, they really had time to sit and ponder what the future held.

"You know, Patrick, I kept the silver threepence piece that you gave me when we said goodbye all those years ago. You said it was lucky. I don't expect you realised just how much you meant to me. I kept your letters for a long time but eventually I was given the choice between destroying them and getting married to Bob. I chose, reluctantly, to burn them, but your memory was never erased, and I continued to hold a candle for you. Now here by some quirk of fate we're together again."

"Well," said Patrick, "What do we do about it? The future is in our hands now. Before, I really had to study so hard and was reliant on my parents for finance, and their approval in the matrimonial stakes too. They were very keen for Elizabeth and me to be married so we became engaged, soon after I returned to Ireland. We had a very happy marriage. Elizabeth was a wonderful wife."

He took a photo from his wallet and passed it over for Lucy to see.

She was beautiful. I see that Sophie has inherited her gorgeous hair and green eyes," she remarked.

"She was a lovely person and didn't deserve the tragic end that she suffered," answered Patrick with a faraway look in his eyes.

"What do you think about Richard and Sophie getting married?" asked Lucy.

"Well, they certainly seem to be very much in love. I have to admit I sensed a little bit of irritation from Sophie, though, at Richard's insistence on postponing the wedding date again, although I do understand how upset Richard must be feeling at all the untimely events within his family. I hope it's of no consequence."

Lucy felt rather disturbed at these remarks but chose not to comment.

The next morning, Patrick took Lucy to the station. Embracing her and giving her a long, passionate kiss, he said goodbye. He had not lost the art! He said he would very much like to meet her again.

Lucy had so much to think about. Her initial reaction was that of pure joy. It must be one in a million chance that this should happen but she wondered whether it was, indeed, wise to allow this deeply held love to be reawakened. She wondered, too, whether it could possibly live up to the memory that she held. Would it be better to let that good memory remain? It would be difficult, bearing in mind that the two families were about to be brought together through the marriage of their offspring. Her heart kept telling her one thing, but her head urged caution. She did think that it would be a long time before Patrick could forget his late wife and had the feeling that, perhaps, she would always live in her shadow.

Soon after Lucy returned, Sandy called. "I was wondering whether you have the time in your busy schedule to fit in a dinner with me tomorrow. It's my birthday and I would very much like to celebrate it with you."

This was like a bolt out of the blue.

"Oh, what a lovely surprise. Thank you. Yes, I'll look forward to that," answered Lucy. "I could do with cheering up."

Lucy spent the rest of the day wondering what she was going to say, if anything, to Sandy about her meeting with Patrick. She had to admit that she still felt quite excited about meeting Sandy. She thought this was strange given that she had not long since met the love of her life. She was aware, also, that she had previously decided Sandy was not for her.

"How was Australia and your recent trip to London?" asked Sandy.

"Oh, it all went off very well. I had a wonderful time in Australia, although it was obviously tinged with sadness after Bob's death. I had a trip to London to meet an old friend. It was exciting too. It has all been such a whirlwind that I have to step back now and try to settle down to work."

Sandy sensed something was troubling Lucy. He thought it better not to pry too much for she had after all had a very trying time recently and he did not wish to be seen as interfering. He desperately wanted to pick up the threads of their earlier relationship but knew he must choose his time carefully. He had made one or two advances towards her which she did not shrug off.

Lucy was in somewhat of a dilemma. She became very contemplative. There was a lifetime of events to bridge since she and Patrick had first met. There were so many obstacles to overcome if they were to resume their relationship. What about Sophie and Richard? What about her work and her studio, which was really beginning to show results for all the hard work that she had put into it? She was not sure, either, that she wanted to give it all up. Lucy could foresee a difficult situation arising. Now she had time to place everything into perspective, the excitement of meeting Patrick started to wane, and Lucy began to feel that the desire was not strong enough to surmount these obstacles. She did not seek another failed marriage.

After Lucy had left them, Sophie noticed that Richard became very quiet and was becoming more withdrawn as each day passed. One evening, when he was about to retire to his study, she felt compelled to ask what was troubling him.

"I was hoping it would pass given a little more time but since you ask, I'll tell you that after much consideration I think I would like to return to England."

Sophie looked aghast. "What's brought this on then? I thought it was South America after your contract has finished here. What about us? What about our wedding and the plans I have for my career?"

"I've taken all that into consideration. I'm not saying it's all over, far from it. Of course, I want you to come with me, but I realise I can't expect you to put your career on hold. When I was packing up my father's possessions in Devon, I had this overwhelming surge of homesickness. The cottage is so beautiful. It's a perfect place for us to start. I'd be closer to mum too. She's been through so much. She's coped stoically, but I'd like to be on hand to give her a bit of support. I know that it means our plans'll have to be put off for the time being. Sophie darling, I do still love you, but I'll understand completely if you don't want to come with me."

"I have a choice, then? Sounds like you or my career. Well, I won't give up my career."

"Suppose I return for, say, six months. It would give me time to settle into a new job and put the cottage in order too. You can continue with the work to which you are committed and think about your next step. After all, at the moment, you're unsure what your next move will be. Maybe you would consider joining me. I do hope so, but I won't put any pressure on you. Perhaps by then, this thing, whatever it is, will have passed and I could join you wherever you might be. Who knows, but my feelings for you remain unchanged."

"That's asking a lot, Richard, after all the time we've spent planning our future. We've put our wedding on hold twice because of your family situation and I don't think I want to do so again. It'd be so difficult if we were on different sides of the world."

"Please, darling, do give it some thought. That's all I ask. I am so sorry."

“I’ll sleep on it and let you know tomorrow, but don’t hold out too much hope.”

Sophie walked calmly from the room. Inside she was boiling. How could Richard do this to her? Her father’s warnings were ringing in her ears.

Sophie went to bed that night perplexed and confused. She could not face Richard the next day, so she wrote him a letter. She told him that he must have had his plans already mapped out before he had even thought of discussing them with her. She understood what a traumatic period he had experienced and was very sad for him, but would have expected him to look to her for support rather than move away. To do what he suggested indicated to her that he was not wholly committed. She thought that trying to continue their partnership when they were on opposite sides of the ocean would take too much resolve. It would inevitably put too great a strain on what was already a delicate situation. She admired his sense of responsibility towards his mother, but she had no desire to take second place.

‘Love does not disappear overnight, Richard, but after much soul searching, and difficult though it is, I think we should call it off. It will be hard to bear but, long term, in both our interests. I do hope you will find another with whom to share your life and who will make you happy. I will always cherish the time we spent together.

Goodbye and God Bless,

Sophie’

Lucy was aghast at receiving Richard’s news. She was both sad and relieved. Sad for them, but relieved for her own situation. She declined Patrick's next invitation to London and tried to explain her feelings in a detailed letter. Lucy never did tell anyone about Patrick and her meeting with him. She tossed out the silver threepence piece. Now all that remained would be a gradually fading memory. Whether this was the best thing, only time would tell. She was startled by the telephone but not surprised to find it was Sandy.

“Hello, Lucy. Hope you don’t mind me ringing but I wonder if you’d like to come out to dinner with me. I’m off again to the Middle East. I think I might be away for some time.”

"It's kind of you to offer, Sandy, but I have rather a lot on my mind at the moment. I'm really not in the right frame of mind for farewell dinners. Why don't you go to the golf club for a few drinks with your pals? They'll be better company than me."

"Perhaps I could cheer you up."

"Thank you, Sandy, but the answer is 'no'. I have received news that Richard and Sophie have broken their engagement. Richard is coming home and will be staying with me for a short time before going to Devon."

"All the more reason why you should come out and not stay at home brooding over something that you can't change."

"The answer remains the same, Sandy. We've spent some wonderful times together. Let's not spoil it now by having an argument. I just want to be left alone to get on with my painting and grow my business. Please try to understand. It's not easy. This really is goodbye. I do hope you have a good trip. Thank you for everything. I wish you every happiness."

Sandy was at a loss for words.

"Thank you. Goodbye," he managed and put down the receiver.

He had tried hard to win Lucy but, despite his love for her, he decided that it was time to give up.

Richard returned and, after a brief spell with his mother, settled into his late father's cottage which he had decided to keep on for the time being. He managed to get a transfer with his company within travelling distance of his new home. His secondment in South America was put on hold for two years. Lucy was delighted that she was able to see more of him, but her workload and the distance kept her from visiting too often. At least he was in this country. She was careful not to mention Sophie. She knew what he was going through. He would bring up the subject if he wanted to talk about it.

***

Lucy's business thrived. She found time to paint and occasionally exhibited her work.

The next two years passed so quickly. Richard was leaving to take up his secondment. She went down to his cottage to spend his last weekend in England with him. While there, she took the opportunity of visiting Plymouth Arts Centre. She was looking critically at some of the work when a familiar face came into focus. It was Pip. Despite the unpleasant incident, she was pleased to see him.

"Pip, of all the people I should bump into."

"Lucy, how good to see you again. I'm so pleased that you're still prepared to speak."

Lucy's face broke into that all familiar, captivating smile.

"Yes. I have put the past behind me now. Let bygones be bygones. You're looking well. Do you have any exhibits?"

"No. I've come out of interest to view some paintings of Scotland by a contemporary. I'm not sure whether you're aware that I had a number of trips up there to paint. Hey, there's a lovely little cafe on the premises. How about we have a coffee and a chat?"

Lucy, a little tentatively, accepted the offer. They had a lot to talk about. Pip explained about the wonderful support he had received, which had helped to get his life back on track again; how painting continued to be a source of comfort to him. It seemed that he had had a complete metamorphosis. Lucy, who had always been at ease with Pip's company, prior to the untimely incident, began to let her initial guard fall as that sense of tranquillity once again began to creep over her.

From that chance meeting, their love of art had once more brought them together. They continued to meet and to visit art exhibitions regularly. And so, over time, they mended the broken threads of their once beautiful friendship.

Acknowledgements
I would like to say a special thank you to family and friends and everyone, who either directly or indirectly, helped make my publishing dreams a reality.

A great appreciation to Oliver Eade, who gave generously of his time, and without whose continued support and encouragement my book would not have been published; to my daughters for taking time out to correct spelling gaffes and sprinkle commas everywhere; to Tony Parkinson for his recommendations on the choice of cover photograph from my amateur photographic attempts and for his recommendation of FPfooteprint; and to FPfooteprint of Jedburgh for their cover design.

Author

Patricia Goodwin was born in the South of England but has spent most of her adult life in various parts of the North, mainly in Yorkshire. She started writing for pleasure, after retiring from a long and varied career in nursing, teaching, running her own hotel and latterly nursing home.

Nine years ago she moved to the Scottish Borders to be closer to family. Here she joined the Borders Writers Forum and Kelso Writers.

She writes stories for young children, adult fiction and memoirs. Autumn in August is her first novel.

Printed in Great Britain
by Amazon

50229078R00094